THE BIG BET

Too Much Action

Owen B. Greenwald

EPIC
Press

Too Much Action
The Big Bet: Book #5

Written by Owen B. Greenwald

Copyright © 2016 by Abdo Consulting Group, Inc.

Published by EPIC Press™
PO Box 398166
Minneapolis, MN 55439

Cover design by Candice Keimig
Images for cover art obtained from iStockPhoto.com
Edited by Ryan Hume

LIBRARY OF CONGRESS CATALOGING-IN-PUBLICATION DATA

Greenwald, Owen B.
Too much action / Owen B. Greenwald.
p. cm. — (The big bet ; #5)
Summary: The team's fragile truce with the Mafia has been shattered, and they are
in big trouble. They've been left with an ultimatum: pay their debts in cash, or in
blood. Naturally, Jason would rather pay cash. With the discovery of an underground fighting ring that may not be as fortuitous as it initially appears, it offers an
opportunity to raise money quickly.
ISBN 978-1-68076-187-0 (hardcover)
1. Swindlers and swindling—Fiction. 2. Deception—Fiction. 3. Young adult
fiction. I. Title.
[Fic]—dc23
2015913150

For Amanda L. Aguilera,
who was there when I faltered near the end
and motivated me as I muddled through
that final stretch

ONE

SHIFTED FOR THE THIRD TIME IN A MINUTE, TRYING TO find some tree that didn't dig its bark into my spine like treasure was buried there. And for the third time that minute, I was disappointed. Trees just weren't designed for sitting against. I added that to the list of *Things Wrong with the Outdoors* I'd been compiling since we'd arrived at Central Park. Next time Kira suggested we meet outside, I'd have an irrefutable argument ready—proof against all claims of beautiful days, skies that hadn't been this blue in months, and precious hours we were wasting not exposing ourselves to Mother Nature's imperfections.

Yes, *this* is the quality of argument I suffer through.

Like, *at least* bring up Wilson's biophilia hypothesis, or Berman's research on the effects of nature on cognitive ability. Sure, those arguments had counters, but at least I'd have to *think*. But if your thesis reads like *Oklahoma*'s opening song, don't be surprised when it remains unconvincing.

Besides, what's so great about the outdoors? It can't even get chairs right. Humans figured them out *eons* ago.

But I'd been outvoted, three to one (Addie, at least, had been wearing an appropriately apologetic expression), so here we were, soaking up the early afternoon in Central Park alongside families and tourists. As always, we were discussing subjects of a highly sensitive nature, but there was room enough in the park for everyone, and as long as Addie (who was keeping lookout) warned us in time, we could seamlessly switch our topic to the McRib. We didn't whisper to each other, or form a huddle, or take any number of basic security measures—that only draws unwanted attention in public settings.

Consider it from your perspective. You're not gonna care what some random teens're chatting about, but if they're wearing face masks and looking suspiciously at passers-by, you might get interested.

Us? Not at all suspicious. Four recent high school grads with bright prospects. And, less visibly, blood on our hands.

I was trying not to think about that.

Our target was Deborah Callahan, a well-traveled art enthusiast with a taste for the old masters. Her bimonthly exhibits were always well-staffed and secure, but Kira'd managed to obtain the security overview, and I'd found a few potential holes. We were still in the Frame phase, but it could be our most high-profile caper yet . . . and our most lucrative. As long as people sold stolen artwork on the black market, there'd be wealthy eccentrics looking to buy with no questions asked.

Of course, there was another reason I'd chosen her—her upcoming exhibit's largest donor was none other than Jorgensen International. Lucas always *did* have a polymath's taste for art. The question of how much he knew about my activities'd perplexed me ever since we'd caught his agent tailing us in DC. If he knew about this job, he'd have a vested interest in stopping us.

And if he *did*, his tactics would answer my *other* big question about Lucas Jorgensen, which was, has he decided he wants me dead? Richard certainly had, and evidence pointed toward their working together.

I should've gotten an answer out of him before it was too late.

Anyway, I'd gotten stricter about picking jobs lately. Our tenuous peace with the Mafia, now three months old, wouldn't survive any intrusions on their domain. And with our last enemy taken care of—well, I'll call it what it is, *dead*—I was trying to avoid making new ones. Life's easier when you don't have to spend it looking over your shoulder.

Those were two of my three constraints—jobs couldn't overlap with Mafia business or make new enemies. The third was a secret from the others—nothing that required violence.

This wasn't just a reaction to what I was carefully *not thinking about*, though it certainly hadn't made the decision harder. My concern was Kira. I couldn't trust her around the possibility of a fight.

I didn't wanna give her the enjoyment, the *positive reinforcement*, the dark joy of causing pain. Not since her non-reaction to Richard's death. Not since my suspicions about the fate of the Mafia's hit team that she'd "scared off." Not since last Saturday, when I'd gone to the boxing regional championship and seen the twisted, grim enthusiasm in her smile as she beat her opponent into the mat for the gold without even breaking a sweat.

No, Kira was unofficially sidelined for now. In fact, *none* of my strategies for dealing with security, if they discovered us, involved beating them up. I'd put many hours of thought into working around that constraint.

So naturally, the first thing Kira said after she saw

the plan was, "Why can't I just punch their faces in and stuff them in a closet?"

She said it so casually, so innocently, you could almost miss the *desire* behind those words.

I'd thought asking her to decrypt the file I'd found on Lucas's computer might distract her from her resurgent bloodlust, but when I'd tried to find it again, it was gone. Deleted. Just one more piece of the equation keeping me up at night.

"If the alarm's raised, step five becomes almost impossible," I said smoothly. I *didn't* mention the ways step five could've been improved to account for that, and I hoped Kira wouldn't suggest them. She was, I'd been realizing, far smarter than she pretended.

"So I'll take them out so quick they can't make a noise."

"And if someone randomly opened the closet and found them?"

Kira rolled over onto her belly. I almost flinched away involuntarily, but she just propped her head up on her elbows to look down at my notes, then shrugged. Placated. For now.

Addie was wearing a foreboding look that Z and Kira thankfully didn't notice. She was the only one I'd shared my suspicions with.

"I'm not even surprised," she'd said glumly, and then she'd sat down and said nothing for almost a minute.

We'd agreed telling Z wasn't the best idea right now, given that Kira was maybe the only thing keeping him around, and definitely the only thing keeping him civil. Besides, neither of us wanted to have that conversation. *Hey, Z. Did you know the girl you like's a total psycho?* It wouldn't end well.

He *had* to've noticed, though, the way she smiled whenever Richard was brought up. Some of the loudest arguments'd been between Addie and Z about whether what we'd done was necessary. I found myself agreeing mostly with Z, but I never got involved directly. Kira usually didn't either—wouldn't wanna drive Z away—but she never quite managed to keep that grin off her face.

This whole situation was just so fucked up.

I didn't even understand my own reaction. Like, Kira was one of my best friends, so my revulsion made sense on a personal level. But from a practical standpoint, it shouldn't have changed the capacity in which I used her. I'd been willing to have her hurt people *before*. Did it *matter* if she enjoyed it more than she should've? The people were getting just as hurt either way. Hell, this way, at least *someone* was getting some endorphins. From a utilitarian perspective, it was *better* this way.

But it still squicked me out.

"Yo, can we wrap this up?" said Z suddenly, looking at his phone. "I got something else lined up."

"What?" I asked.

Z shrugged. "Friends," he said, and I could tell he wasn't planning on getting more specific than that.

I gave him my most irritated look. "We planned this meeting around *your* schedule, dude, seeing as it's suddenly so full. You said you could spare two hours."

"Well, something came up, alright?" snapped Z, suddenly hostile.

It wasn't alright. This'd been the *fifth* day I'd suggested. Z'd shot down the previous four without going into detail, probably just to be annoying. That, or he was playing dominance games. I'd finally managed to find a day he said worked, and he was gonna blow me off anyway.

But it wasn't worth the fight.

"Yeah, whatever," I said. "Double-check your calendar next time, okay?"

Z gave me a thumbs-up. "See y'all later," he said to the group, and then, "Bye for now," to Kira, who gave him a warm smile.

I let out a long, frustrated breath.

"You're just gonna let him ditch?" asked Kira. Her tolerance for Z's antics dropped sharply when he wasn't around.

I shrugged. "Better to just not engage him. He'll get tired of it soon."

Addie ran sympathetic fingers through my hair, and I noticed it actually *was* a remarkably bright, clear, beautiful day. The dark cloud over my mood cleared somewhat and I took in a deep lungful of air.

Z was nearing the center of the field, growing smaller and smaller in the process. Something jiggled at my brain as I watched him, some observation that refused to be filed away without telling me something important . . .

I blinked. "But he came with *us.*"

We looked at each other as if to confirm that yes, he had.

"So . . . he had a spare car parked here, then?"

"I guess he'll flag down a cab," said Addie, following the trajectory of my gaze to look at Z's retreating back. "Or his friends are picking him up."

Z's innumerable friends. Knowing him, he could probably hitch a ride with a bosom buddy he'd met playing hopscotch in first grade. It made sense for a guy with that many friends to be in high demand. It'd never mattered *before*, but he'd liked us more back then. Backing off from us and spreading his time more evenly fit my mental model of Z just fine.

But just because something fit the facts didn't mean you accepted it as true. You had to try to disprove your hypotheses, and fail. Perhaps multiple times, if need be. Because if your hypothesis was falsified even once, your model of the world was incorrect.

And something about Z's recent behavior was . . . *off*. Maybe it was nothing, but double-checking cost me little.

I grabbed my notebook off the ground. "Well, he was vital to the plan," I said, letting genuine disappointment into my voice. "No point in sticking around without him."

Addie looked skeptical. "Just go over our parts. We can fill him in later."

I shook my head. "No point. Trust me here."

Trust me here was Addie-exclusive code meaning *I can't currently talk freely*. We'd worked it out for situations exactly like this one. And yes, I had similar-but-different phrases with Kira or Z. Because you can never be too prepared.

Addie caught on immediately. "If you say so."

"Goddammit," sighed Kira, picking herself up and brushing bits of earth off her pants. "Now what do I do with my afternoon? Well, I'll drop you turkeys home and—"

"Hey, this is a *great* time to go on that date in the park we've been talking about!" Addie interrupted, looking hopefully at me.

I sighed heavily, because that would've been my normal reaction. "Could we move the venue somewhere more . . . indoors?"

Addie smirked. "Nope."

"Alright, alright, I see how it is," said Kira, mock-offended. "No one wants to keep Kira company. Poor Kira, the under-appreciated chauffeur, the endlessly-sacrificing bosom friend . . . "

The possible serial killer.

"I knew you'd understand."

"Whatever. See you bitches tomorrow. Addie, Skype tonight?"

"Sounds good. See you online."

We said our goodbyes and went our separate ways.

Addie and I took turns sneaking glances behind us to make sure Kira was really leaving.

"Alright," said Addie once Kira'd left hearing range. "What's going on?"

I motioned her along in the direction Z'd gone. I couldn't see him anymore, so I started walking faster.

"Let's see what Z's up to."

TWO

"**Y**OU THINK HE'S UP TO SOMETHING?" ASKED ADDIE, matching my stride.

"I dunno what I think."

"What about your gut?"

"Gut feeling's an unreliable method of generating hypotheses," I said distractedly, keeping my head rotating, doing wide sweeps, looking for Z's full head of dark hair above a dark green T-shirt.

"I know," said Addie, somehow packing a litany's worth of exasperation into two words. I just *knew* she was rolling her eyes even if I couldn't spare a moment to gather corroborating evidence by looking. (The irony was not lost on me.)

"Right now, our dataset matches multiple explanations," I said. There was a small hill ahead and I made for it, breaking into a light jog. I could afford to look undignified if the alternative was failure—vanity's a wonderful thing, but never to success's expense. "So we're gathering more."

"Got it. And then we determine which explanations no longer fit. I'm not a *freshman*. I've got five explanations. You?"

I considered. He could be telling the truth, deliberately keeping his distance for personal reasons, trying to annoy me, selling our secrets—*or* otherwise betraying us, but those were the same thing, really—or . . . "Four," I admitted, and Addie smirked triumphantly.

"He might be too far already," she pointed out as we neared the hill.

She was right, unfortunately—with his head start, we'd need to slow him down to have any hope of catching up. How to do that with only a wallet, a phone . . .

That wasn't even difficult. I speed-dialed Z.

"What's up?"

I consciously maintained my pace. People naturally slow down while multitasking—it's the brain's way of making space to do two things at once. Like walk and talk, for example. You could keep going at speed if you focused, like I was, but Z had no reason to do that. Unless he was in a hurry . . .

"Hey man, you in a hurry?"

"Kinda. You need something?"

"Uh, yeah." Not losing speed was hard as we started uphill, but I leaned into my strides and moved doggedly forward, almost robotically. "We're just brainstorming ideas, and we wanted to ask—shut *up*, Kira—yeah, if anyone you know can access the building's blueprints."

A short, thoughtful pause. "I got a cousin in City Hall. And a couple friends who . . . you sure that ain't just public info? Or could Kira get it outta the system?"

We reached the hilltop and I squinted down at the people dotting the surrounding area. Z could've easily been one of the more distant figures, but my eyes were refusing to just *see farther*. The summer sun's harsh glare forced me to squint uncomfortably as well. Why did people *enjoy* the outdoors?

"I'll get back to you on that."

"There," said Addie, pointing a long finger, "on the bridge."

The blob on the bridge wasn't displaying more Z-like qualities than any other distant blobs, but I trusted Addie. "Let's go."

"What?" said Z.

"Uh, nothing. Hey, wanna meet up for dinner later? We're feeling Chinese, but if you've got a craving . . ."

"Maybe. Don't count on it, I might be busy. Not sure."

I racked my brain for some way to extend the conversation further, but the natural progression was, "What're you busy with?" And that'd be a bad move. He could get suspicious, or defensive.

I finally settled on "Okay, let us know," which I immediately realized was suspicious, because my natural inclination really *was* to ask what he was busy with. If Z knew me well enough, *not* asking would be suspicious.

But if he'd noticed something amiss, he didn't show it. "Alright, will do. Bye."

"Bye." *Click.*

Ahead of us, the little human-shaped blob accelerated. Addie and I followed abreast, gazing ahead with the same intensity young couples usually reserve for each other's eyes. We maintained a safe distance, but never lost sight of him again.

At Central Park West, he hailed a taxi—one of several loitering in wait for passengers. We easily caught another before his made it more than a stoplight away. I had a wad of twenties ready in case the driver needed convincing before he'd follow another car, but he reacted to my demand with an acquiescing stare, which made me wonder how common that request was.

Traffic was stagnant as ever, and punctuated at frequent intervals by blaring horns—the serenade of the Big Apple. We crawled forward inch by inch, always keeping Z's taxi square in our sights. We weren't very subtle, but Z had no reason to suspect he was being followed . . .

My phone chose that minute to ring and I half-thought it'd be an annoyed Z who'd just, in fact, seen us. But it wasn't.

"Report."

"All three fronts just checked in. Nothing out of the ordinary." Derek's voice was low and smooth, with a quiet self-assuredness that commanded respect. He'd probably paid a vocal coach handsomely for it.

As I said, we had peace with the Mafia. Theoretically, this meant our families were safe. But nobody who actually cared would think *theoretically* good enough, so I was still paying Derek's teams. In an emergency, we wouldn't have time to re-hire them—we'd need them already in position.

Besides, Lucas's accounts were practically bottomless, so I wasn't exactly *wasting* money.

I said what I always did during these every-twelve-hour reports. "I have no additional orders at this time. Continue your watch."

"Yes, Sir," said Derek, managing a hint of irony—just enough to be noticeable while still retaining plausible deniability. *You may pay me,* he was reminding me, *but I have the expertise, and if I give an order, you will listen.*

Well, he *was* right. "Thanks, Derek," I said, and hung up. We'd awkwardly exchanged hello-goodbyes at first, but the cold demands of efficiency'd stripped them away. We had our standard model now, and by following it, we both had a couple more minutes in our incredibly busy lives.

People aren't machines, said Lucas's voice in my mind, as arrogant as he always was in the flesh. *But treat them like they are, or they'll start thinking they can have ideas.*

Sociopathic "advice" from an asshole, that's all. Maybe someday, I'd be able to block it out entirely, but it'd only been getting louder lately. He'd drilled his lessons into me all too well—and during my formative years, too. He'd known what he was doing, I'll give him that.

One night when I was little, I'd been watching the *Buffy* movie in our TV room. The vampires'd just killed

Merrick, and as they turned on Buffy, I'd been rooted to my seat, utterly enthralled.

Then the movie'd paused and Lucas was standing in the doorway. I dunno how long he'd been there. "Tell me," he'd said, "what did the vampires just do wrong?"

It was an easy question, especially since my movies were often interrupted like this. "They let her live."

In those days, I'd still felt a spark of pride for getting the right answer. For passing.

"Lothos had his enemy beaten, and decided to let her go *because she wasn't ready to fight him yet.* You've seen enough movies to know how this ends for him. All because killing her wasn't worth his time that second."

He hadn't turned on the lights, so his face was dark, his outline barely visible. "Finishing a weakened enemy is *always* worth your time," he said. "Remember that well, my son. There's nothing so slow to forgive as someone you've crushed, and nothing more thirsty for vengeance."

Then he'd let me finish, but now it was pointless

because he was right, I *did* know Buffy was gonna kill the vampires, and the entire plot was ruined anyway.

I didn't have many favorite movies growing up.

That particular advice kept drifting through my head these days. I'd left Richard alone after cheating and extorting him, and that mistake'd almost killed us. The Bonannos *were* another loose end, for all the peace we'd made. They wouldn't forgive the trouble we'd caused them, not soon—the police crackdown was still in full force and another den'd been raided just last week.

If I'd actually learned my lesson, I'd listen to the Lucas-echo and *do something*—before something was done to *us*.

And yet . . .

Yes, we'd gone after Richard and "finished" that enemy . . . and the memory still sickened me. It *didn't* feel like the right choice, whatever Lucas would've thought. And really, if Lucas *did* approve of something, that was strong evidence against it. I'd known that since *before* I'd started suspecting he wanted me dead.

"I am not you," I muttered, not caring that he couldn't hear.

Addie's eyes flicked up. "What?"

"Nothing," I said quickly. "Just thinking out loud."

Some part of me'd made the call to eliminate Richard, the same part that'd made sure I couldn't reconsider. The same part that'd discarded alternatives as unworkable or impractical. The part that'd internalized Lucas's fatherly wisdom, for better or—hell, who was I kidding—worse.

My phone buzzed again, but it was only a text from Kira.

use pertecton :)

I grimaced and shoved it back into my pocket.

I wouldn't let myself become another, smaller Lucas Jorgensen. It's a fear of mine, sometimes, that I'll wake up someday as cold, bitter, and hateful as him.

The drive continued across the Madison Avenue Bridge, and our intrepid driver stuck to Z's taxicab like glue all the way across without issue. We crossed I-87, which meant Z was *probably* headed into the Bronx.

And still, they didn't seem to notice us following.

As we entered the South Bronx's residential district, the streets grew narrower and more pockmarked, the gardens smaller and scragglier. Ahead, Z's taxi slowed to a halt. I slid the closed privacy screen open. "Two more blocks."

"Okay," said the driver amiably, and he swerved around the other cab.

"Is it just me?" said Addie, looking out the window, "or is this a really not-good part of town?"

It wasn't just her. Unkempt yards and peeling paint were the prevailing aesthetic, and the gutters appeared lightly dusted with broken glass. Then again, Z *did* have friends literally everywhere.

We pulled over to the curb, where I gave our driver a handsome tip for his no-questions-asked approach to driving. Once he'd left, we walked back along the street to the building Z'd stopped in front of. The entrance was open . . . but decidedly uninviting.

"Think someone'll shoot us if we go in?" I asked.

"Definitely. Let's not."

I agreed with her assessment, which only made me wonder more what Z was doing here. Maybe they *were* his friends, nothing more. But the whole situation smelled funny, and I wasn't leaving without an explanation—mundane or otherwise.

We decided to wait for him to reemerge, which had the twin benefits of not involving trespassing, and avoiding an awkward situation if Z'd actually walked into a different building altogether and'd just pulled up by this one for convenience. The opposite house was surrounded by a low brick wall, but neither of us wanted to risk incurring someone's wrath by sitting on it, so we stood instead, trying to look like locals. We talked club business to pass the time, and when that ran dry—after nearly an hour—started doing impressions. Addie's were invariably of higher quality, but she never stopped assuring me I was doing a great job.

It was while she was doing an impeccable imitation of Mr. Appargus, our old principal—involving a great deal of sputtering and gesticulation—that a solitary figure emerged from the open door. Addie cut herself off mid-sputter.

It was Z, looking proud as hell.

THREE

WE STOOD IN PLAIN VIEW AS Z WALKED DOWN THE blue-painted steps onto the sidewalk. He gave the street a quick once-over, passing over us momentarily. Then his head turned back sharply, smile vanishing, lips a puckered O of surprise.

"Long time, no see," I said casually.

"The fuck're you doing here?"

"I was just, we were—"

"—Going on a date," said Addie, so naturally *I* almost believed it.

Z looked pointedly at the dilapidated houses lining the narrow roads, then at the garbage-strewn sidewalk strips. His surprise was rapidly replacing itself with anger.

"So we've been nicer places," she admitted.

I heard the *click* of a gun being cocked and a large man stepped out the door behind Z with all the deadly grace of a stalking panther. Some people're obviously bad news—and this guy was the *Challenger* explosion. His face was contorted into a truly fearsome scowl, the effect of which was enhanced by the Glock pointed my way.

This time last year, that would've phased me, but I was almost *used* to having guns pointed in my direction. I couldn't simply stifle the (very reasonable) fear that it'd be used to poke holes in my fragile, fleshy body, but my brain had several anecdotal reference points to reassure itself that things'd turn out OK. The disarming, thought-scrambling shock, like jumping into freezing water, had lost its power over me.

"There trouble here?" said Mr. Bad News, not looking away from us. I smiled grimly back.

Z hesitated. "It's cool," he said. "They're friends."

Mr. Bad News spat and backed inside again, not breaking eye contact until the door slammed shut.

Z crossed the distance to us in five long steps. "Cut the bullshit, you ain't on a date. Tell me what the fuck's going on, or I'll—"

"What're *you* doing here?" I retorted. Addie touched my arm, which meant I should shut up and let her talk, but I ignored her (which I regret only about eighty percent of the time). "This looks like a dystopian movie set."

Z shifted uncomfortably. "Just seeing friends, like I said."

"In your own words, cut the bullshit. Your *friend* just pulled a gun on me. What're you here for, dude? Pulling a job?" A thought occurred to me. "You turning on us? Finding some thugs to bump us off, is that it? Are you—"

"*Jason.*"

It was mostly the surprise at hearing that much force emerge from Addie's small mouth that shut me up.

"You shouldn't've followed me," said Z.

"Well, we did," said Addie. "Might as well own up. There are no secrets between us four, you know that."

I had to bite my cheek hard to keep from snorting with laughter. Z was staring pointedly at me with a small smirk and I knew he was thinking the same thing.

"We know something's up," said Addie, undaunted. "You've barely been able to meet with us lately. Something's going on we don't know about, something big. And it involves the sketchiest house I think I've ever seen."

You could've balanced a pail of water on Z's head without spilling a drop.

"I know you aren't betraying us," continued Addie. "Partly because that's not *you*. Jason knows that too—he was just speaking impulsively. You have convictions that the rest of us just don't, and I don't think betrayal's something you'd consider. But also because you wouldn't have sent your friend away if you *really* wanted us gone."

Z's next words came from a place deep inside him so far removed from the usually-spoken that by the time they'd reached his mouth, they were tired and barely audible.

"I'm not that guy."

"You can tell me, Z," said Addie, motioning me back. I complied—only an idiot would interfere with the magic that was Addie persuading someone.

She stepped forward and took Z's hand. "We're friends. We won't judge, I promise."

Z turned away wordlessly and started walking, away from the house and down the sidewalk. He pulled Addie behind him, not seeming to care that she still clung to his hand.

"I'm not who you think," he said as we crossed onto a new block. "Not the guy who knows you gotta pick right over wrong. Not the guy who helps his friends along that path too. Maybe I was, once. A kid. A dumbass. That guy'd never chase after revenge. But he hadn't lost a dad either."

He kicked out savagely at a telephone pole, then shouted in pain. We gave him space as he sat on the curb and wiggled his toes, making sure nothing was broken.

"I get it now, why y'all can make the choices you do," he said as he wiggled. "I never thought I could hurt someone just because he hurt *me* . . . but what happens when the hurt's *inside* you, stabbing whenever you breathe? And it stops being something you feel, and becomes something you *are*? You can't just forgive him, right? You gotta get even. Because it ain't fair he ain't feeling that. Y'all get it, right?"

I nodded dumbly, lost for words. I'd never seen this side of Z before, and didn't trust myself to say the right thing to whoever he'd become.

It was Addie who spoke, blessed Addie, who *always* knew what to say. "What did you do, Z?"

Slowly, through shaky, uneven breaths, the whole story spilled out.

"I set everything up," he said softly, making sure nobody was close enough to hear. "Made my own plan. These guys here, they're Crips. I knew them from school and I've been coming by for a while. They know me, they listen to me . . . *fuck*, man, I don't wanna do this to them, but I *gotta*—"

"What—" I began, but Addie motioned me silent, and, after collecting himself, Z started again.

"I talked them into raiding the Latin Kings. They're pals with the Bloods, so it was an easy sell. They don't fuck with the Crips too much, but their Blood ties're enough. And I got together with a friend in La Raza, worked out a weapons deal, because La Raza wants the Kings gone. The weapons convinced the Crips that didn't wanna do it before."

On my list of things Z was likely to do with his friends, *incite them to gang warfare* was at the bottom. Or *would've* been, before now. Had his anger changed him so much?

But I still couldn't see the *point*, besides causing

mayhem, and Z wasn't a cause-mayhem kind of guy. There was no angle.

"Promised the Crips I could get the Kings leaders in one place. Just now, I told them. And I know the place because I helped set it up. I . . . " He hesitated longer than usual here. "I heard from my friends in the Kings."

If anything on that list was below *incite them to gang warfare*, it was *get them killed*. I felt chills down my spine imagining Z cheerfully chatting up his Latin Kings buddies, pumping them for information, then catching a taxi to the Bronx and selling them out . . . I caught Addie's eye, and saw similar trepidation there.

"I set that up too," Z continued. "The meet with the Kings and . . . "

But then he looked at me and all but swallowed his tongue.

"Alright," I said, picking my words carefully as I continued processing this flood of information. "You've instigated a Crip raid on the Latin Kings.

But I don't understand *why*. You trying to take over the gangs or something?"

"No," said Addie. "That part wasn't important—it's all incidental. He almost told us the important part, but stopped himself. He doesn't think we'll like it." She just smiled at Z's resentful look. "Sorry, but you're *really* easy to read."

"That just ain't fair," he muttered, and I privately sorta agreed.

But what *was* he doing? Not betraying us—that'd been a stupid guess, even I had to admit—and *probably* not restructuring New York's underworld on a whim. But he wouldn't say more . . .

I looked at him and he stared defiantly back.

But I'd already guessed it. He'd let slip he wanted revenge. To get even. And while I wasn't sure how the rest fit, only one target made sense given *that*, and that same target *would* piss me off. But he couldn't be *that* stupid . . .

"Lorenzo Michaelis," I hissed. "You *didn't*."

Z froze, practically confirming my suspicion, and dread rose in me like a tide.

"You're mad," said Z quickly. "But I've worked everything out—"

"The fuck're you thinking?" I whisper-shouted. "Yes, I'm mad, I'm pissed as hell! We don't go after the Mafia—we have a truce, and if you break it—"

"Nah, this is all me. He made that truce with *you*, and—"

"And we're known associates. You think Lorenzo'll *investigate* if we helped you? He didn't become the boss by giving his enemies the benefit of the doubt."

"I started setting this up right after I quit," said Z defensively. "By the time I joined again, it was way too late to back out."

That'd been months ago. Addie and I'd stumbled into a plan *months* in the making. "You set up . . . what, exactly?"

"Fine," said Z. "I talked the Latin Kings and the Bonanno family into dealing with each other, alright? They're meeting to finalize the details soon, and I know where. Lorenzo's gonna be there. In person. You know how rare that is?"

" . . . And you've just given that place and time to the Crips, but neglected to mention the Mafia's involvement. The Crips show up, hit the place, and Lorenzo hopefully ends up dead in the crossfire," said Addie. "Damn. That's . . . pragmatic."

Which was just a diplomatic way of saying *callous*. Z flushed, but didn't back down. "I'll have cops standing by too. It'll be harder for the gangs to figure out what happened if everyone's in jail. Like I said, I've been planning this for months."

"I don't care if you were *born* planning it," I said. "It's too risky. If even the slightest thing goes wrong, we're fucked. You're calling it off. Now."

"I can't." Z didn't look even slightly sorry. "The meet's *happening*. If there's no raid, the Mafia's gonna walk out twice as strong as before."

"I don't *care*," I said firmly, trying to clamp down on my panicked anger before it started dictating my actions—it wouldn't serve me in this situation.

"We're at peace with the Mafia, so I don't care if they take over the whole damned city. You break our truce and it won't matter how weak they are, because they're strong enough to kill us all if they decide it's worth it. We're living on a knife's edge!" I practically yelled. Addie put a finger over my lips and I took a deep breath. "You're gonna walk back in there and convince them to call it off."

"Yeah, *that* ain't suspicious," mocked Z. "I come out, talk with two shady-ass teens, then go back and cancel everything. Plus, the only way they'd scrub the mission's if I said I was lying. I think you can figure out why I ain't doing that. *Plus*, they'll dig if they're suspicious, find your identities. Put the pieces together. And maybe sell you out to the mob anyway, for trying to use them as weapons."

"But *we* didn't—"

Z shrugged. "I don't think they'll see it that way. And you *really* don't want these guys as enemies."

I clenched my jaw in frustration. "You son of a bitch."

Z just shrugged again.

I wanted to *scream*.

The Mafia is the enemy at your back, said Lucas in my head. *They will strike first if you don't.*

"And you shut up," I snapped without thinking.

Z frowned, confused. "I didn't say anything."

Just what I needed, to start arguing with imaginary voices. Might as well check myself into an institution now. At least there'd be family.

"I *did* think this through," said Z, still infuriatingly calm. "Nobody's gonna suspect us. It'll be written off as gang violence, and the Mafia'll be too busy with the Crips to bother poking around. I sketched this over like, *months*—it's solid."

Gang violence. That's what they'd call it when Z's friends were tricked into shooting each other just so Z got his shot at revenge. I called it cold as hell. At least when I'd used the same strategy against Richard, I'd used two enemies against each other. Not people I called *friends*.

Besides, something about this whole plan set my teeth on edge, some wrinkle I didn't see . . .

But Addie was nodding at me, and it's not like I had a *better* way out of the fucked-up situation Z'd put us in, so I held out a hand. "Alright. Just this once, then you leave the other plans to me, or I fucking *swear* . . ."

Z grasped the hand and shook tightly. "This all goes well, I'll never wanna make one again."

FOUR

N THE WAY HOME, I MADE THE MISTAKE OF THINKING the day couldn't get worse. As any student of dramatic irony could tell you, this was a bad move.

But it shouldn't *matter*. The universe doesn't run on dramatic irony. My thoughts don't *actually* affect external events. At least, that's what I'm gonna keep repeating to myself, because remembering days like this almost convinces me otherwise—illogical as that is.

Cerebrally, I know there was no connection between that thought and the day worsening. But I *did* think it, the day *did* worsen, and a weak, under-evolved part of my brain saw connections that didn't necessarily exist.

Addie and I spent most of the drive bouncing thoughts off each other, mostly about how to minimize the fallout of Z's stupid plan. All we'd really managed to agree on by the time we reached her house was that things could go wrong *so many different ways,* it'd be impossible to avoid them all. I spent the drive home narrowing down the likely failure points so I could at least have an *idea* of what to expect.

I also couldn't get over how *cold* Z's plan was. Even if it went perfectly, he'd be blatantly betraying friends—which he'd always decried. What'd these past few months been *like,* that they'd changed him so entirely?

These thoughts swirled together, never quite coalescing into a coherent mass. They occupied my mind all the way up my driveway, onto the porch, and through the Jorgensen estate's massive double doors. I was so focused, I didn't hear Jeeves's usual greeting cough and he almost blindsided me. A half-second before we collided, I noticed him and jerked to a halt.

"Hey, Jeeves. How's it going?"

I wasn't trying to start a conversation or anything, just observing basic social niceties on my way upstairs. But Jeeves apparently hadn't gotten the memo, because he stayed right where he was.

"Hello, Master Jorgensen," he said in his fake (but impeccably accurate) English accent.

He was looking at me strangely. If I'd paid more attention, I could've figured out what was happening, but I was still preoccupied with thoughts of gang warfare, so I just stepped around Jeeves—and promptly skidded to a halt again as he followed me left, blocking my path.

He coughed his stupid proper butler's cough.

I tried again, but he was just as quick the second time, and his cough was somehow even *more* obnoxious. He touched my chest softly, but I felt the threat behind it—though he rarely shows it, Jeeves is actually pretty tough. Kira'd noticed his stance straightaway and later told me she thought it'd be fun to spar with him.

"I'd win, of course," she'd said. "But he'd last a while."

It'd been amusing then—the image of the family butler fighting for his life against a young woman who hadn't even started college. That same butler holding his hand against my chest in a casual reminder that he could break both my wrists if he thought Lucas would approve . . . was *not*.

"You wanna talk about something?" I asked.

Jeeves coughed again.

"My apologies, Master Jorgensen, but Mr. Jorgensen was adamant that you no longer be permitted on the premises."

"*Excuse* me?"

For one confused moment, I felt sure I'd misheard. But the more my brain processed what I'd heard, the more I had to admit I'd understood perfectly.

If I'd been thinking more clearly, I'd have seen this coming.

"He told me it was high time you were gone from the house, making your way on your own merits," sniffed Jeeves. "You were told originally that you would no longer be welcome after graduation, so you had plenty of time to make alternate arrangements."

God dammit. I'd hoped Lucas'd forgotten he'd said that. When he hadn't followed through immediately, I'd allowed myself to hope . . .

But Lucas doesn't forget things.

"It's been more than a month since then," Jeeves continued. "Your father—"

I felt a flash of annoyance.

"—feels he's been more than reasonable."

I raised you to always be prepared, I heard him say in my mind, picturing his schadenfreude-filled smile (his favorite facial expression). *And somehow, you still haven't learned.*

I wasn't even mad he hadn't given me notice—I've come to expect that shit from him. What *really* pissed me off was, he'd sent his fucking *butler* to deliver the message. Because his fucking *hedge fund* mattered more than me.

But then, I guess I've come to expect *that* from him too.

"I'm sure he does," I muttered. "Alright, fine, I get it. I'll grab my stuff and—"

"Mr. Jorgensen was clear that if you don't leave immediately, I'm to have you removed."

"But my stuff—"

"He didn't mention it."

His voice, while still crisp and professional, had an undercurrent of apology that made hating him impossible. It was just his job, after all. *He* wasn't the one throwing me out—just Lucas.

"Lemme talk to him," I said. It almost stuck in my throat coming up, but I forced it out anyway. It was all I could think to do, my one chance of buying myself a few days. I'd negotiated with Lucas before. There was a chance . . .

Jeeves folded his arms across his chest.

"Mr. Jorgensen is very busy right now, and indicated he could not be disturbed."

Of. Fucking. *Course.*

Not only could Lucas not be bothered to evict me himself, he couldn't even free up his oh-so-important *schedule* to hear me complain about it.

But I knew he wasn't bluffing about security tossing me out. And that meant Jeeves wasn't either. I didn't feel like suffering another indignity right now.

"Well, that's that," I said, feeling hollow. "At least I won't have to see that bastard anymore."

Jeeves huffed at me (as was usual whenever I bad-mouthed his employer), but I'm sure he understood my perspective.

"Bye, Jeeves," I said. "Thanks for all your help over the years."

"Goodbye, Master Jorgensen," Jeeves said stiffly. "Good luck."

It *stung* losing the only home I'd known for eighteen years. I'd never thought I'd miss it, or the smug asshole that'd had it built. But it'd been a convenient base of operations, housed a security team I trusted implicitly, and . . . it'd been home.

Now I didn't have one.

The taxi was gone, of course. It wasn't *that* far to the gate, but it felt like forever. I followed the winding driveway past the artificial waterfall, past the lemur cages, past the welcoming daffodil arrangements. Despite his limited space, Lucas really *had* done everything he could to create a country estate within New York City's borders.

The black, wrought-iron gate buzzed open at my approach. With a deep breath, I stepped off the Jorgensen estate's grounds. Free.

Without a living space, security, or hired help—but free, nonetheless.

At least I didn't have to worry about getting my stuff back . . . because it was in a large pile of furniture and boxes on the sidewalk two dozen yards away. A few people were eyeing it speculatively—there's no way it was all still there. I jogged over, uprighted my swivel-chair, and sat sentinel over the rest, pondering my options.

No getting around it—I needed somewhere to stay. And, more immediately, to move my stuff.

The obvious answer? Call Kira.

I hesitated, hand already in my pocket. Did I really want her involved? With how erratic her behavior'd become? With how unsafe I'd felt around her lately?

. . . But those were silly worries. A little discomfort couldn't erase four years of friendship overnight. And I *did* need her help. Her violent tendencies couldn't possibly come into play moving *furniture*.

Besides, not like today could get worse, right?

FIVE

"SOMEONE ISN'T HOLDING UP HIS END," GRUNTED KIRA.

I gritted my teeth and heaved the couch as hard as I could. It rose slightly and I took another step down the hallway before it could drop.

"Better. I should've carried this one myself."

The couch blocked my look of skepticism, but I like to think Kira could feel it.

Somehow, we made it without my muscles giving out. I buzzed my door open, hefted the couch again, and together we walked it down the short hallway to the living room, which was bare save for a coffee table and several large cardboard boxes. We dumped it unceremoniously in the middle.

The room opened onto a beautiful view of the city from forty-six stories up. Not a place for the agoraphobic . . . or the poor, for that matter. No one-room flat for Jason Jorgensen, but a full upscale apartment on the Upper West Side.

Not the best money could buy—a bedroom, bathroom, and small kitchen made up the rest of my scant living space and washing machines were communal—but I hadn't had much choice on such short notice. In the coming weeks, I could shop around for my perfect apartment. This one'd simply been the nicest currently available (and owned by a landlord willing to expedite the process for extra. Money talks. Eloquently). While I'd confirmed I had the cash to cover every charge he introduced (some of which I'm sure he'd invented on the spot), Kira'd shopped around for the more necessary pieces of furniture. Her taste was deplorable as always, but I appreciated the gesture, and I could always redecorate later.

"Wanna move it now?" asked Kira, looking around

the white-walled room appraisingly. "The more shit we dump, the harder it'll get."

"Let's grab the rug," I suggested. "Then we can place them both at once, in case they need to overlap."

I'm in charge of the thinking for a reason.

"Huh?" said Kira. "Why not the bofa?"

"The . . . bofa?"

"Bofa these *nuts!*" crowed Kira, pointing triumphantly at her crotch.

And that's prime evidence for why Kira *isn't*.

"Thanks, by the way," I said on the elevator ride down, for like the hundredth time. I just wanted her to understand how badly she'd yanked my ass out of the fire by swinging by with her dad's truck with so little warning.

She was still the most steadfast pillar of a friend you could hope for, whatever other messed-up shit she was dealing with. As long as you had a back to have, Kira Applewood would have it. I valued that immensely.

But showing genuine emotion around Kira's always a gamble, so I'd never told her. Maybe she'd appreciate it.

Maybe she'd get embarrassed. Maybe she'd decide that wasn't the impression she wanted to give and change her behavior entirely. That kind of unpredictability's why I stick with airy banter. Banter's safe. She feels at home there.

The rug fit nicely into the center of the windowed living room, and we decided the couch belonged against a side wall—I'd seen enough action movies to know sticking it by the window was tempting fate.

"Wanna move those boxes?" I indicated a stack of two that stood between the couch and its decided home. Kira flashed me a thumbs-up and grabbed the sides firmly.

"Pussy."

I couldn't help but marvel at Kira's frame as she lowered, and then lifted, her knees. Her deltoids bulged out over her shoulders, tapering smoothly into her upper back beneath the gray tank top. In moments of exertion, you could *see* just how much muscle Kira was packing. It wasn't usually noticeable unless you looked closely—Kira'd never cared much for building size. It was strength she was after. And I'd seen what those arms could do in the ring, whether bulging and veiny or not.

That muscle wasn't for lifting boxes. It was killing muscle, lean and vicious. Meant to win fights, not bodybuilding competitions.

Physically, Kira was a combat machine. Was it any wonder her mind matched up?

In my mind's eye, I saw a Kira five years from now, one who killed for the rush it brought her, who widened her criteria for victims to keep up with an ever-increasing demand for the feeling of ultimate power, the power over life and death—

"I'm concerned."

Shit. That'd been out loud.

Kira, taking slow steps, walked across the room and put down the box. Only then did she turn around. "Why?"

"Nothing, I guess."

Kira stared at me unblinking, and I knew I'd have to say something to get her to turn away. If I didn't, the seasons would turn and New York would crumble around her as she stood resolutely awaiting an answer.

"Addie," I offered at last, hoping that was enough to divert her.

Kira's expression softened. She gestured at the couch. "Wanna talk?"

"Nah," I shrugged. And then, realizing there actually *was* something I wanted to talk about . . . "I mean, sure."

I flopped down onto the red-checkered cushions. Kira sat next to me and put a hand on my arm, wearing a generic, fits-all-situations, comforting expression.

"It's complicated. Weird. Like, you know how she and Z keep arguing?"

"Yep. She's gotta stop that. You know how tough keeping him around is?" Kira smiled proudly. "Don't pretend like you're surprised—you get it."

"Yeah, I do. And I don't think—"

"But enough about me. Back to you. What's up with Addie?"

"It's, well, she seems really convinced setting Richard up was the right move."

Kira nodded slowly, exaggeratedly. "Uh-huh."

"We talked right after it happened." I didn't need to clarify what *it* meant. "I was frightened she was gonna break up with me or something for devising that plan, for making the call. I didn't know if I could live with it, that decision. And then she said I was right. There wasn't a better way."

Kira was still looking nonplussed as to my point, and I was only now realizing what I should've realized before I began—though we were friends, she was unlikely to be a sympathetic ear.

"But she didn't *convince* me, is the thing. She just got me not thinking about it. And that should've been my first clue—when someone doesn't want you thinking about something, it means they're arguing for the *wrong side*, don't you see? The right side doesn't have anything to *lose* from people thinking harder."

Kira was suddenly regarding me like a beneficent king might look upon a subject he'd just kissed the forehead of, only to learn said subject had an incredibly contagious disease.

"Now she and Z keep arguing, and . . . well, long story short, I keep agreeing with him."

"Agreeing?" said Kira acidly. "With that limp-dick?"

"Limpness of his dick aside, he's making sense," I argued. "The point isn't whether it was necessary or not, it's that we decided we could make that choice. That we could weigh people's lives like that."

"Hold the fuck up. You're saying 'we' like we *all* made the plan, instead of just you."

"Nobody shot it down."

"Nobody's ever had to. We *trust* you, dude—well, Z doesn't, but fuck him, he'll listen to you anyway. You know the path to victory, and you thought having the Mafia waste a shitstain was it, so I'm not gonna argue."

Disputing that was really hard when I just *knew* Kira'd recite my argument back at me next time she wanted to disobey an order.

"And y'know what?" said Kira loudly, "I'd do it again. It solved the problem, solved it one hundred percent, and permanently. You gonna sit there and judge me?"

"That's not why you'd do it again." The words were out before I could help myself.

"The fuck does *that* mean?"

"You *believe* that, I bet, but belief can be a subconscious process to justify positions you're not comfortable holding. What did you think first?" I hurled the words at her—a dam inside me'd broken and I couldn't stop the accusatory flood. "Did you think killing Richard sounded good, or that we needed a solution that was one hundred percent *reliable and permanent?* How many of those solutions did you *look* for?"

Kira's whole face'd frosted over, and her gaze could've pulverized stone.

"And that's the thing about Addie's arguments," I snapped. "They're all excuses for lazy thinking. And Addie's not a lazy thinker, so she's doing it subconsciously. There's something inside her she's afraid to face, and *that*'s what I'm worried about."

"That's *her* fucking business."

"Like it's *your* business that you really like hurting people? Is it—"

Pain blossomed in a black supernova behind my eyes.

Over the next few seconds, I became aware of something hard pressing against my cheek. On further examination, I determined it was the floor. Why was I down *there*?

The answer came slowly, trawled up from the depths of my molasses-slow brain. Kira'd hit me.

She'd *hit me*.

I twisted my head and stared up at her. She was looking down with barely-suppressed dark rage, and her hand was twitching in a way that made me wonder if she was strong enough to break the reinforced glass of my apartment windows. I decided the answer was *definitely*.

She was my friend. She wouldn't do that. But I hadn't thought she'd hit me either.

A trickle of fear dripped down my back, and my brain went into survival-mode. I glanced around wildly for potential weapons, saw only unpacked boxes, and realized it wouldn't matter either way. Kira could make me eat just about anything I could expect to find in an apartment building, even with one arm tied behind her back.

Diplomacy then.

I tasted copper, so I must've bitten something. My lip, or cheek, or—

"You don't fucking get it," snarled Kira. "Addie does. She's too good for you, you fucking *dumbass.*"

She took a step forward, but the flash of anger was already dulling into some unreadable, hopefully safer, emotion.

"Kira . . . "

Kira shook her head and let out a long frustrated sigh. But she didn't come closer. I felt frozen to the ground, worried I'd provoke her if I moved.

"I gotta go," she said flatly. "Good luck unpacking."

She left my field of vision. A few seconds later, I heard the apartment door slam.

That . . . was probably as near an apology as Kira was capable of.

I touched my cheek gingerly, then spat red all over the wood. It hurt, but not as badly as the fact that my best friend'd done it.

Former best friend, I amended. Because I could never look at Kira the same way again. Not without being constantly on guard, watching my every word.

If I could, I'd put her on leave from the group. But I doubted she'd take that well. Or leave whoever told her unharmed. Or even listen at all.

On the bright side, if she snapped one day and killed us all, it'd probably be faster than whatever the Mafia'd do to us if they discovered Z's stupid fucking plan. Which was enough to focus on without adding *this* into the mix.

When it rains, it pours, right?

Still holding my cheek, I went into the kitchen and rinsed my bleeding mouth.

SIX

ADDIE ARRIVED TWO HOURS LATER.

She didn't knock, of course—she never did. One moment I was elbow-deep in a box of clothing and the next I was sitting on the red-checkered couch with my arms wrapped around her. How I'd made the transition, I didn't know.

"Kira said you were having a rough time," she said.

I couldn't parse that at first, but then had to hold back a bark of laughter. "Yeah."

It was too much. You didn't sock someone in the face, say they don't deserve their girlfriend, and storm out only to *call that girlfriend* and send her over. That didn't even *begin* to make sense.

Unless you were Kira, apparently.

"I can't believe he didn't give you any warning," said Addie, blazing with righteous indignation. "What did he even expect you to do? And what happened to your *face*?"

My cheek was swollen where Kira'd struck it, and still pink-red, though the bleeding'd already stopped. Mouth wounds rarely stayed open long.

"I think my face's why Kira sent you," I said. "Lucas is an asshole, always has been. I'm over it—I'm surprised he gave me this long, actually. But this cheek's a genuine Kira special. Extra cheese."

"*Kira* did that?"

I shrugged. "It was just a matter of time. She didn't tell you anything?"

"No," said Addie, suddenly looking very worried. "She wasn't this bad before."

"Well, she is now," I said. "She seemed sorry, though. Anyway, she left me to finish all this unpacking myself . . . care to help?"

"Don't derail me. Kira *hit* you. She's never done

that. If she's getting worse, we need to be prepared, and that means talking."

"We can talk while we work," I said. "It'll be fun and relaxing."

"Well . . . " Addie sighed. "Alright, let's multitask. Which box first?"

I waved a hand at the seven boxes scattered haphazardly around the couch. "Pick one, I don't care."

Addie considered the array, finally indicating the one at her feet. "What's in here?"

"Books, I think," I said, but she was already opening it.

"Huh."

Somehow, from that *huh*, I knew *exactly* what she'd found.

Out came the first, a golden plastic cup on a faux-marble base. And then the second, a pewter cast of a boy on rosewood. And then four more.

"Look at *this*. My boyfriend Jason, a secret jock." Addie's eyes sparkled with mischief.

"Yes, very funny, put them back and—"

"This is a whole other side of you! How many trophies did you win? Do you still sneak out at night and win them in secret?"

"You'll notice the most recent one's from sixth grade," I said sourly. "The year I realized I hated sports so much, even pissing off Lucas couldn't keep me playing. He *hated* that I was wasting my time kicking a ball around a field. But I hated it more. So I guess he won."

Addie laughed and I joined in. I guess it *was* pretty funny now, all these years later. Time'd dampened the memories of eighty-nine-cent hot dog snacks, watered-down Gatorade, chlorophyll-stained stretchy black shorts, and the complex system of carpools I'd had to fabricate so Lucas couldn't just order Jeeves not to take me to practice, and which'd taken *hours* every week to update and maintain.

Sometimes, in my more benign nightmares, I wake up tasting that watery Gatorade.

"And yet you kept them all."

"Playing the long game. Someday he'll visit me here and see them on the mantelpiece."

Addie rotated a gold-plated soccer ball in her hand, casting light around the room. "On the mantelpiece, you said?"

"Like hell I did. I'll put them out special for him, but there's no way I'm—" I caught her wrist as she ran past me, arms full of trophies, and she tumbled into me, laughing. "—displaying those pieces of shit under normal circumstances."

She squirmed comfortably against me. "You win for now," she murmured, and I knew then I'd wake up to find those trophies displayed prominently on the mantelpiece one day, no matter how well I hid them.

. . . Actually, if I could see *that* coming, Addie was likely planning something else . . .

"Do I wanna know?"

Addie shook her head and kissed me. "You didn't enjoy *any* of it? As an exercise of skill?"

"Oh, I sucked. Never had any skill to exercise.

You know, everyone got these, but they would've withheld mine if they could. I actually don't have my fourth grade trophy because the team stole it after the award ceremony."

"I see why you quit," said Addie. She didn't even bother hiding her amusement.

"Well . . . there was *one* thing I liked. The winning, even if *I* was never responsible for it. I understood winning was good, even the first year I played. Lucas made sure I understood *that* much about life."

I grimaced. "I always did like winning. But I dunno if it's really *me*, or Lucas's parenting. Sometimes I think of myself as a sort of Frankenstein of all the traits Lucas thought'd make someone successful, grafted onto a baby year by year."

I realized I was holding Addie tighter. She was responding, shifting the mood of her body within my embrace from playful to supportive.

"I can hear his voice," I admitted to the back of her head. "Sometimes. Not now. Lessons he tried to drill in. And I'm never sure whether to listen—it's his voice, but it's my brain, you know? But sometimes it feels like he's got a mic in there."

He actually *was* talking right now, telling me that opening up like this wasn't safe, but Addie didn't have to know that—it just would've worried her. And I was shrugging him off pretty easily this time. Sometimes it's hard to tell what's safe to disregard.

"I don't wanna become him," I said. "But I feel like I'm already there sometimes. Like the voice *is* me, and I'm in denial. And someday, I'll start listening and take over Jorgensen International and stomp any moral sense I ever had into dust."

"You won't," said Addie. "You aren't like him."

"You've never even met him."

"I can just tell, okay?" she said firmly. "The man you describe is nothing like the guy I'm sitting on right now. I wouldn't be dating you if you were. Won't you trust my judgment?"

"I had a mom, too," I said.

It wasn't an admission I let myself make often.

Addie didn't respond to that, leting the silence

build. She'd asked about Mom a couple times near the beginning, but'd gotten the hint pretty quickly and let the matter drop.

I *don't* like talking about it. I'd only brought it up to get her to back off.

"I, I wish I believed you. But I feel myself changing. Like with Richard, when—"

"Jason," said Addie sharply. She twisted around to face me and the force of her stare fixed my head in place. "You are *nothing* like your dad."

"But how can you *know*? You're telling me what I wanna hear, which I appreciate—"

"Because I—"

Something cracked in Addie's face.

There's no better way to describe it. On one level, *nothing* changed. There were the same hard green eyes, the same stern narrow lips, the same jutting chin. But there was new vulnerability too, a softness behind the mask so tender it left me feeling unclean, like I was reading someone's secret diary,

Addie's every muscle was taught with tension,

ready to spring. Her breaths came faster, more force-fully. And was that . . . *resentment* in her expression?

"I, um."

Her eyes dropped to my chest and fixed themselves there.

"I have a secret."

"You do," I said. It wasn't a question. It'd be stupid to pretend I didn't know. I'd seen it from day one, made it my goal to solve whatever mystery lay at Addie's core.

It was why I'd fallen for her.

She nodded unhappily. "And it's how I know you aren't like him. It's . . . because you aren't like me."

I frowned, struggled to parse her meaning, and then—

Wait, no, that couldn't be right—

"You *care*," she said. "You try not to, but you do. And I . . . it takes a little more effort every day." She was still staring obstinately at my chest, and I couldn't see her face. I took her hand and squeezed it, because I wasn't sure what else to do.

"And I wonder what happens when it takes too much, and I just," a deep breath in, "stop. I feel like I—well, I don't know how your dad feels, but it must be like how I do when I'm not *trying*."

"What do you mean?"

"I—I'm not sure I can explain. It feels like nothing at all. Detached. Like, uh, looking at a riverbank from beneath the river. It just doesn't seem real. Unless I force myself to make sense of it, say that blur is a tree, that one's a fisherman, et cetera. Does that make sense? No. No, it doesn't."

"No, it doesn't," I admitted. "But I'm trying to understand."

Addie shrugged. "Well, it would if you felt it. I wish I had a better metaphor."

"That was a simile, actually." I was going for a laugh. I didn't get one.

"If you don't feel that way, odds are you're less like him than I am," she said. "So stop worrying. That was my point. I didn't mean to . . . whatever this was."

"It's fine," I said. "Hey, you don't worry either. You're nothing like him."

She smiled sadly. "You don't know that."

"You're cuter, for starters."

That got a laugh. A tiny one, barely more than a cough, but I'd take it.

"And you *do* care," I said firmly. "I've heard you talk about your mom. And there's me. I think."

"There are exceptions," Addie admitted. "You're, well, easy to care about."

Luckily, she still wasn't looking at my face so she couldn't see my involuntary smile of relief.

We stayed like that for I dunno how long, but I didn't release her hand.

"It's why I chose to do this," she said abruptly. Hesitantly. "Be with you. Having another person to care about helps keep me grounded."

"Is there a reason you shouldn't? Be with me, I mean?"

She shifted uncomfortably, and didn't answer.

I wasn't sure why Addie's body language was

suddenly so readable, but I wasn't gonna waste the opportunity. "Besides you thinking you'll turn out like Lucas?" I pressed.

Addie sighed in resignation. "Fine. It's just . . . not going to work out, okay?"

It was like she'd just kicked my heart while wearing iron-toed boots. "I think it's going pretty well," I managed through the rising horror, trying to pinpoint what'd gone wrong—

"It is! Which is what makes it so . . . " She sighed again. "Okay. You know how I get hunches occasionally? How I just *know* something?"

"You shouldn't rely on—"

"I'm *never* wrong," she said forcefully. "Never."

That seemed highly unlikely, but I didn't say it. Addie already knew I'd be thinking it, so there was no point.

"That first time I kissed you? After the poker job, at Kira's? Remember?"

"How could I forget?" It was the confusion I remembered most of all—Addie's lips just *barely* lingering on mine, and then, just as suddenly, not. Her flirtatious attitude fading to friendliness almost instantaneously.

"I, uh." Addie was fidgeting again in a most un-Addie-like manner. "I got a bad feeling from that kiss. The worst I've ever gotten. I knew right then, things would end badly."

"But I wouldn't—"

"I know."

Something didn't add up. "But if you trust your hunches, and they say I'll hurt you . . . why stay?"

Addie looked up then, and I saw that her face'd hardened in determination. "Like I said, you help keep me grounded. I kind of . . . well, I *really* need that right now."

It made sense, from a survivalist perspective. Between the vague future threat and the clear, present danger, there was only one correct choice. Addie was rational enough to see that.

Not to mention that in my estimation, the future threat didn't exist. I'd *never* hurt Addie, no matter how many gut feelings warned her otherwise. They were unreliable, untrustworthy, and in this case, flat-out wrong.

They *had* to be.

"At least I'm forewarned," she shrugged. "I can take it. No matter what you throw at me, I'm ready."

"I . . . I promise I won't hurt you. Ever. Emotionally, physically—whatever it could be, I won't do it." It seemed almost too obvious to bother saying. But it felt right. And it meant something to her, too. I could tell.

"Thanks," she said with a tiny smile. "I'll hold you to it."

I lay back and she settled into the crook of my arm, both of us gazing at the ceiling—toward the future, however uncertain.

SEVEN

DIDN'T SEE KIRA OVER THE NEXT FEW DAYS. Z EITHER,
for that matter. I let official business slip.

I needed a fucking break.

Addie brought over what Kira'd driven off with,
and we slowly found places for everything. For such
an expensive apartment, there wasn't *actually* much
room—the living room had easily the most space. I
ended up storing lots of stuff in the kitchen, since all
I really needed there was a fridge and a microwave
(my culinary "skills" meant frozen meals almost every
night). I tried to keep the bedroom uncluttered, but
lost that battle once Addie brought *her* things in—we
hadn't discussed that, but I had no objections. I

ended up giving her the closet off the hallway, but the living room closet stayed mine.

Neither of us mentioned what we'd talked about the day Kira'd lost control. I think we were both pretending that conversation hadn't happened.

It was stupid—obviously it *had* happened. I remembered it, I knew she remembered it, and I knew she knew I remembered it. But that's how people are. They skirt around things they don't feel like confronting.

Speaking of not confronting things, I stopped working on the Callahan caper. The exhibit wasn't for another couple weeks, so things could be put off until tomorrow . . . or the next day, or the next, and so on. That was *some* fallacy, but I couldn't remember which. Eventually, I admitted the job wasn't holding my interest anymore. Thankfully, Addie supported my new outlook and made sure I stayed busy with other things.

It was *hard* giving up work cold turkey. Sometimes I'd absentmindedly pull out my notes on Lucas and try making sense of them. If the art heist wasn't happening, I'd need another way to decipher his motives.

Eventually, I'd remind myself as I shoved them aside.

Maybe (okay, *definitely*) it was stupid, ignoring a possible threat like that. But somehow, I couldn't bring myself to care—even when I realized I was no longer protected by his security. If Lucas *did* want me killed for whatever reason, forcing me into an apartment was a great first move.

But worrying about that sounded an awful lot like work. And he'd probably wanna wait a little either way—it'd be suspicious if I turned up dead mere days after leaving the Jorgensen estate. I could deal with *that* later too—and the thing about *later* is, it's never *now*.

The only business I stayed up-to-date with was Derek's twice-daily calls, simply because *he* called *me*. I eventually started resenting my phone's ringtone, but I knew the reports were necessary, so I picked up anyway and mouthed his unchanging account along with him.

Three days in, the *Times* ran a front-pager about a multi-party gang war. The NYPD'd managed to defuse an all-out gunfight between the Mafia, the Latin Kings, and the Crips. Eight people'd died before they'd controlled the situation. I wondered if any were Z's friends—but I didn't ask.

Z texted me the day after. Three words. Lorenzo got away. I didn't bother answering. I didn't care what'd gone wrong, so long as Z knew he wasn't allowed to try again. That was Addie's job. She'd know how to say it diplomatically, and I was on break.

That break stretched on two more days—two days of shopping and trying to cook and watching so-bad-they're-good movies with Addie and generally having the life I'd always privately ridiculed. As I drifted to sleep that second day with Tommy Wiseau's hammy acting reverberating in my ears, the last thought that percolated through the dreamy haze of tiredness was that maybe I'd just *never* reconvene the gang. No more Frames, or Ops, or even Revels. I'd retire and go into marketing—which was a stupid thought, but one my tired brain found acceptable.

My phone woke me at six a.m.

"Fucking shit," I slurred, reaching over Addie's sleeping body. It took three tries, but I eventually managed to grab it and focus my bleary eyes on the screen. A snapchat from Z. I was fully intending to fall back asleep once I'd opened it.

I saw the pic. I read the text.

Then I reconvened the gang.

EIGHT

Z WAS SHAKING. HE'D BEEN SHAKING SINCE I'D arrived, and I didn't expect him to stop anytime soon.

The truce is broken.
The price is one million per head
or your life. You have two weeks
from this day to decide
or we will decide for you.
Expect us.

The words gleamed wetly in the morning light.

"What's the chance that *isn't* blood?"

"I really, really, really don't wanna think about that," muttered Z, as Kira said, "It's blood."

She wasn't looking at me, which I was fine with. "One more time," I said. "You woke up, turned on the light, and saw the words on your door?"

"And snapchatted you three, yeah," said Z. His gaze kept flicking back to the message. "It was right there. I didn't even *wake up*. I shouldn't even be . . . Fuck, dude. Fuck."

It shouldn't have happened. I wasn't paying four mercenaries full-time to guard Z's house so people could walk right by them and leave messages *in blood on his wall*. I briefly considered the possibility that our security'd betrayed us, but there wasn't much evidence either way, so I resolved to pursue the matter more intently before I left. I needed to know that I could rely on Derek and his team—otherwise, what justified the price tag they commanded?

"The truce is broken," Addie recited. "Unless there are other truces I'm unaware of, that refers to the mob. And they aren't happy that one of us took action against them."

Z was very deliberately avoiding her eyes.

"What that doesn't explain," she continued, "is how they figured out who was responsible."

"They shouldn't've!" Z exploded suddenly. "I was careful. I worked everything out." He rounded on me. "Tell them. It was solid."

I hesitated. I wasn't gonna agree since his plan obviously *hadn't* been solid, but at the same time, there'd been no glaring flaws that begged to be pointed out . . . But there *had* been one, somewhere, or Z would've been safe . . .

So make it a puzzle. Look from the mob's perspective. Given the details of the plan (call that the input) and the result (call that the output), what sequence of events linked them? What steps would *I* have taken following the attack? I already knew the result—Z's being implicated—so if a solution led *there*—

"Oh," I said with a sudden rush of realization. "You were the common link."

Z looked like he wanted to take a swing at me, and since I'd had enough of that recently, I decided to explain.

"Pretend you're the Mafia," I explained. "You're negotiating with the Latin Kings when the Crips attack, then the police swoop in and arrest everyone who's not dead. It's a disaster. Lorenzo Michaelis is mad as fuck. He resolves to figure out what happened. He interrogates people from every faction involved, trying to determine who betrayed his position to the Crips. He gets stories from everyone involved, including La Raza. And when he puts them all together . . . there's one common element. One guy who was talking to *everyone*."

I looked meaningfully at Z.

"We know the NYPD's untrustworthy," said Addie. "It could get back to Lorenzo who tipped them off. That leads back to Z too."

"*Everything* does," I said. "Safe to assume he's the mastermind. And he's a member of this gang that caused us trouble before, so they've obviously broken the truce. Let's kill them all."

Z was breathing hard and his fists were balled in

helpless anger. I clapped his shoulder. "Nice going. We're fucked."

Only a Herculean amount of self-control kept back my *told you so*.

"Could be worse," said Kira.

We all looked at her in disbelief.

"They're giving him an out. A million a head. How many heads we talking?"

"There were seven people there," said Z. "Seven million. In two weeks. I can have some of the—"

"Sure," I said. "I'll help you out. We've got two million left from the Treize caper. That leaves five."

"So we've gotta find five million dollars in two weeks?"

"No." I shook my head. "You do."

I saw Addie and Z opening their mouths to object, so I plunged on. "This is *your* fuckup. We were done with the mob, and you brought them back down on us. We'll help you, because the CPC watches out for its own, but you gotta fix this. Make it right."

Z's face crumpled in anger, but I held his gaze.

Sending him a message—*we're your friends, but don't take that friendship for granted.*

Finally, he nodded tightly.

"Wipe it off," he said, gesturing at the blood. He was still shaking slightly, eyes kinda wild, and I realized seeing that on his door was like seeing his dad dead in front of him all over again—both courtesy of Mafia intruders he'd been powerless to stop.

A half-hour later, Z's door was clean as ever, and the bloody paper towels were buried at the bottom of the garbage can, wrapped in newspaper and a plastic bag. Even though I knew the blood'd *probably* just been carried in in a bottle, I couldn't shake the image of a grinning mobster opening a vein in Z's bedroom. It was so *obviously* for effect, but that hardly diminished it.

"I gotta move out," said Z for the fifth time. "Get somewhere where if they come after me, they ain't gonna hurt anyone else. My family ain't involved in this."

"Did any of them see the message?" asked Addie,

and Z made a noncommittal grunting sound. This earned him a stern glare, beneath which he became *very* sheepish.

"I don't want them worrying."

"Keeping them in the dark isn't fair," said Addie firmly. "They're in this house with you, and you've put them all in danger. You need to warn them *now*, so they can start preparing. If we wait until our two weeks are up, they won't have time."

Z's face reminded me of a plate that's been cracked one too many times, and needs only one last tap to lose its structural integrity. And when he shook his head, it was with such agonizing slowness, I thought moving any faster might shatter him.

He didn't have to say anything more. I saw that in the way Kira folded her arms and set her jaw, and how Addie turned her hooded eyes toward the ground. We all (for obvious reasons) had done our best to hide our proclivities from our families. No matter the threat, we'd defend that secret. Kira and Addie would've given the same answer in Z's position, and they both knew it.

It'd be an admission of defeat—the ultimate sign we'd gotten in over our heads, were so helpless we could only tattle to our parents and let them take the helm. Childish, maybe, but the kind of childish every teenager's allowed to be.

"I'll make sure they're safe anyway," said Z. "All I gotta do is raise the cash. No problem."

"How?"

It just slipped out. But we'd all been thinking it—*someone* had to say it.

"I have a plan. Second cousin works for a, well, it's tough to explain." Z trailed off, thinking hard. "Kinda like a fight club—" Kira's eyes lit up. She *loved* that movie. "—but with side betting. Or like live MMA, but not scripted. People fight and rich bastards bet on them—it's supposed to be a secret, but all the old CEOs know about it, and they're into some pretty sick shit. I'll go down there, make some big bets, and holy shit Kira, why're your eyes so big?"

"The fuck kinda question is that?" Kira cracked her knuckles. "Ain't every day you learn Heaven exists."

"Your idea of Heaven's betting on illegal fights?" Kira laughed.

"Not what she meant," I said, not looking at her. "No, by the way."

"I'd like to see you fucking stop me," said Kira.

Slowly, deliberately, I twisted my head over and up to stare her in the eye, *willing* her to actually listen for once. I'd let her get away with too much, and it was time to remind her who actually called the shots. "I'm serious."

"*I'm serious,*" she mocked. "You don't tell me what to do, *boss.*"

She practically spat my old nickname at my chin. Her face was growing, expanding to fill the entirety of my vision and I rooted myself, unwilling to give a single inch beneath the pressure of her gaze. That left the pressure with nowhere to go—it could only build and build, and somewhere outside my sightline someone said, "Guys?" But that someone wasn't Kira, so I disregarded it.

"What's the deal? You think I'll get hurt? Like I can't take care of myself? Like I need you and some fancy-ass plan to get anything done?" Her voice rose like a swelling wave on each successive question. Soon, it'd peak.

I squared my shoulders. Bring it on. What was she gonna do, punch me again in front of everyone?

"Chill, guys," said another not-Kira. "My family's asleep, we don't wanna wake anyone—"

"You're out of line. Z's planning to use this thing to save his ass, maybe all our asses, and the last thing he needs is you sailing in and fucking things up because there isn't enough hitting people in your life!"

The wave crested.

"You'll deal with it!" Kira thundered. Rage streamed effulgently off of her in a corona. She would've looked majestic if the overall effect weren't so fucking terrifying. "You stuck-up, self-centered shitcock! You think all I'm good for's fucking things up? You want me to beat people down on *your* schedule? Is it okay when you *order* me to?"

She paused for breath, still seething, and I tried to get a word in edgewise, but my mouth wasn't cooperating. I could only stare into the eye of the storm. But the worst'd passed—Kira exhaled loudly and the room came back into focus. Addie and Z were staring at her, open-mouthed.

"Fuck this shit," she snarled. Her cheeks were mottled with anger, all except her scar, which cut a white streak across her cheek. She took a step toward me and I flinched back involuntarily. Maybe I was getting used to guns, but an angry Kira was *far* more intimidating. It was like staring down a mother bear, but at least you knew a mother bear was protecting its cubs. Kira was completely unpredictable.

And a bear's face could never contort into such a mask of rage as Kira's.

I fought every instinct telling me to run as she approached, but she wasn't coming toward me at all—she was headed for the door.

Z tried to place a comforting hand on her shoulder as she passed, but she whirled angrily and he snatched it back before she could take it off at the wrist.

"I am *so done* with this bullshit," she said between deep breaths. "I am gonna drink until I forget how pissed I am, and none of you fuckers better remind me."

I didn't know it was possible to slam a door *open*, but Kira managed it. We heard her stomping down the hallway all the way out the door, followed by movement upstairs. The commotion'd finally woken someone.

Addie stared after her in wonderment. "It's before noon. It's not even *nine*."

"I'll schedule the intervention," I said wryly, and then, considering, "actually, though."

"Yeah," said Addie. We both looked at Z, who looked like he wanted to argue the point, but he crumbled beneath our looks and sighed loudly. " . . . Yeah."

"Someone's gonna be down here soon, so let's

work this out now," I said hastily as the movement upstairs became louder. "Let's investigate this fight club thing. How's Friday?"

"Nope," said Addie. "My cousins are visiting from Australia, and *Mamá* wants me around. Saturday?"

"Kayla's dance recital," said Z. "That's a no-go. Thursday's the same. Gotta be Friday."

Z and Addie locked eyes, seeing if either'd back down.

" . . . Well, you can manage without me," said Addie when it became clear neither would. "You two go Friday and catch me up. We'll go from there. And talk about Kira later."

There was nothing I'd rather do less than work alone with Z . . . except, right now, work alone with Kira. From Z's expression, he wasn't too happy about the arrangement either. But it made sense to bring the guy who knew the venue.

Footsteps on the staircase—we were almost out of time. "It's a plan," I said. "We can cab together—get me at nine."

Z still looked pretty freaked out, but he gave a nod of assent.

"And *we*," I indicated Addie, "can have dinner Saturday, since you're standing me up on Friday."

"It's not standing you up if I tell you in advance."

"Whatever. Dinner on Saturday. Something nice and formal—should be a nice de-stressor. Besides, we could use a break from trying to eat my cooking."

We'd raised our voices again by this point, now that our conversation was innocuous enough to let it be overheard. Our presence in Z's room this early was still weird—but that could be explained.

"Only you," said Addie tartly, "would rationalize the benefits of a date with your girlfriend."

But she was smiling.

NINE

THE CAB DROPPED US ON A DINGY STREET CORNER IN Long Island City that would've been disgusting even *without* its light coat of garbage, courtesy of the McDonalds across the street. I watched its taillights get smaller and smaller, and tried not to think about how long it'd take for another to arrive if we needed to leave in a hurry.

"C'mon," said Z, beckoning me.

He seemed subdued, less antagonistic than usual. The silence grew between us as we walked, Z looking for some sign only he knew. The longer it stretched, the more unthinkably disturbing it became.

I wasn't in any hurry to. It was kinda nice, not

sniping at each other. If I said something, his response could easily end that streak. It's how he was these days, all hard edges. Ever since the gruesome message, he'd worn it openly—even Kira'd noticed by now.

But *here* of all places, on a nighttime stroll through the City's slums, I could pretend the old Z was back.

He was getting better, though—earlier tonight, he'd even been able to look me in the eye long enough to give me the lowdown on the venue. The boss, a man named Peter Storm, ran several similar "fight clubs" around New York. For safety's sake, meetups were infrequent, and never in the same location twice—but in this warehouse, Peter Storm's fights ran daily and never moved. Z'd heard rumors that his other ventures were just distractions for the Feds to keep away from his business here. Others said he was backed by the Russian mob, but when I'd looked for substantiating evidence, I hadn't found any.

But then, it *would* be buried deep . . . if it existed.

Z stopped abruptly. "This is it."

It was a plain warehouse door, just like any other. I

couldn't see any sort of secret sign . . . though I guess that'd be the point. Regardless, Z stepped confidently forward and knocked a particular pattern against the wood.

The door rolled open. Z turned to beckon me forward, then vanished into the darkened room beyond. I followed him into an antechamber furnished with red couches. The door rolled shut behind us, pushed by a large woman with dark curls, a sharp chin, and a black T-shirt emblazoned with an anchor.

"Good evening," she said.

"Cold evening for a T-shirt," Z observed.

I thought he was bantering, but the woman's demeanor immediately changed. A pass-phrase, then.

"Name?"

"Zahir Davis. You probably know my cousin Ricky." Z jabbed his thumb toward me. "This one's cool."

The woman gave me an approving once-over, then produced a Walkie-Talkie and pressed the *speak* button twice.

"Have fun," she said with a smile, and the far door slid open too. Z beckoned me again.

Before I even walked though, I could hear pained cries from further in, as thick on the air as the smell of cigarette smoke. I did my best to ignore it as I walked through.

The chamber opened up into the warehouse proper, which was far emptier than warehouses generally are. It was pretty dark, but light glinted through the shelving blocking off the rest of the room. Z motioned for me to go left and I followed him until the shelving ended. That's when I got my first look at the ring.

Or at least, the crowd surrounding it. I've never been good at estimating numbers, but there must've been at least fifty, not counting the occasional stern-faced bouncer. Bleachers surrounded them on three sides, but they were almost completely empty—a slow night, perhaps. Occasionally, the crowd would part briefly and I'd glimpse the combatants, brightly lit and shining with sweat, grappling with each other on a bloodstained concrete floor. It looked like the arena's boundaries were dictated mostly by how close the crowd pressed. Or maybe the light—while at least three high-powered spotlights were focused on the ring, the crowd was a formless mass of silhouettes from this distance—probably so people felt less worried about being recognized. I noticed additional unlit lights strung across the girders above, along with several sets of speakers and maybe a half-dozen cameras. This was a major, professional operation. And—as a groan of pain reminded me—their business was pitting desperate people against each other for money.

Z must've caught something in my expression, because he looked sympathetic. "That's just how it is here. Nothing we can do."

Except leave and make the money another way. That was the easy answer. But then, answers that don't actually solve the problem usually are.

"Let's get this over with, then," I said through gritted teeth. "Say I wanted to bet . . . "

Z jabbed a thumb away from the ring toward the left corner of the warehouse, where the most disorganized line of people I'd ever seen—*throng* might've been more accurate—had gathered.

As we approached, the gloom became less oppressive and I could make out a long row of piled-up cardboard boxes, behind which was a tall, slender man with a wispy mustache. He was carrying on simultaneous conversations with three different people.

"That's the official bookie," said Z. "I dunno how he calculates odds, but he's definitely gonna rip us off. This is his day job and he's gotta make a profit. Everyone else here, maybe they'll bet. Some're throwing around serious cash. But I figure the best bet—no pun intended—is going official. They'll play fair no matter what. That's worth getting a worse deal because private bets can turn ugly pretty quick. We don't have the firepower to come out on top if that happens, so official channels only. Safety's important."

I raised an eyebrow.

"Relative safety," Z amended.

Loud cheers erupted from the crowd around the ring, and a wave of triumphant bodies surged toward us, eager to claim winning tickets. A winner'd been decided, and those who'd bet on him were, by extension, winners themselves.

But now I was imagining some hardened community veteran flying off the handle at something we said or did, or how much money we'd won. How easily one could pull a knife and find the soft tissue between my ribs. That'd be the end of me, genius or no genius. It finished sinking in that Kira wasn't here to interpose herself between me and that hypothetical attacker. The only person watching my back in this dangerous, unpredictable place was Z . . . so I'd probably be on my own.

"I wish Kira were here," I muttered.

Z's perfunctory agreement sounded almost *wistful.*

"She'd probably fuck something up though," I said quickly. "Hell, she'll fuck something up anyway. Just wait—something'll go wrong and it'll be her fault."

I turned away, examining the listed "odds of the day," which doubled as a match schedule. Three-to-two, five-thirds-to-one, and other such ratios adorned the dimly-lit sheet of butcher paper, next to the combatants' names, the fight's parameters, and the times they were scheduled to compete. Going by the odds, at least, everyone seemed pretty evenly matched. The longest odds I could see were seven-thirds-to-one in favor of someone named Los Tiburón.

"Holy shit," breathed Z. "Fifteen-to-one."

He pointed down the sheet toward the middle, where my eyes'd started skipping. Sure enough, there it was—"Diamondback" versus the under-favored "Queen Bitch." *Damn*, those were ridiculous odds. Either Diamondback was *very* good, or Queen Bitch was the fight club equivalent of a redshirt.

"They don't usually schedule matches that unbalanced," said Z. "It's no fun watching someone get curbstomped for forty-five seconds."

By now, we'd reached the impromptu desk. "Seems like safe odds," he said, handing the bookie a wad of cash. "Two hundred dollars on Diamondback, please."

As the bookie handed him his ticket, there was a

hushed gasp from the crowd, followed by an uneasy silence.

"That the next match starting?" I asked, but Z shook his head.

"They just came into the ring. They'll wait about ten minutes, stretch, feel each other out, you know. Gives us room to bet. But we ain't betting big today, right? Just casing the joint?"

"That's right," I said. Next to the fifteen-to-one odds was a time in military hours (22:00) and the word *surrender*.

It was almost ten now.

"Who do you think just came in?" I said. "Diamondback, or Queen Bitch?"

"Probably both," said Z. "They generally come out together. Usually you get more cheering though."

Later, I'd ask Z exactly *how* he knew so much about the underground fighting scene. As we shoved our way through the tightly packed circle to a better view, my brain was positively *bubbling* with possible explanations . . . all of which promptly flew away as, through a gap between two relatively still members of the arena's audience, I got my first look at one of the combatants.

It was Kira.

She was smiling, carefree, hair in two tight braids, wearing a simple black tank top and shorts. She stood at ease before the crowd, not going through warmup exercises or even sizing up her opponent.

"Motherfucker," said my mouth, while my poor overloaded brain attempted to process the anger that'd suddenly flooded it—anger at being disobeyed, anger at myself for not seeing this coming, anger that Kira'd be left in a bloody heap on the dirty warehouse floor and I could do absolutely nothing about it, or even muster an *I told you so.*

"What's up?" said Z, and then he saw too. He sucked in his breath sharply. "Mother*fucker.*"

I had to stop this, there had to be a way, they'd *never* let a teenager fight . . .

Somewhere above me, a speaker crackled to life.

"Attention, attention. The ten o'clock fight begins

in three minutes. Diamondback versus newcomer Queen Bitch. Finalize your bets."

This wasn't a prank, or a game. This was serious—maybe deadly.

The speaker was probably in the small off-the-ground booth at the back of the warehouse, where the fourth set of bleachers should've been. There were definitely people inside, illuminated by their machinery's blinking lights, and their window and vantage point gave them an unparalleled view of the action.

"She'll be fine," said Z, sounding like he was trying to convince himself. "These don't go to the death. She'll take a few hits, bow out, and that'll be it. We can chain her up or something."

"Wouldn't stop her."

"Right."

"Don't worry, I'll think of something."

But three minutes later, when a shrill sports-whistle began the match, I still had nothing even resembling a plan, and Kira and Diamondback, a hulking man in his late twenties and already balding, came to blows.

They traded punches faster than I could follow, but their first sortie was over in seconds and it was Diamondback who'd disengaged with a quick step back, rubbing his arm just above his elbow.

You could *hear* dozens of people simultaneously realizing their bets weren't as safe as they'd first assumed.

I pushed my way closer to the fight—not wanting to watch, but unwilling to miss a single second of the action. Z followed close behind, helping me work my way into the crowd's inner ring.

"If she survives, I'm gonna kill her," I muttered.

They closed again just as fast as before, adding kicks and shoulder-blows into their tactics. But it was Kira's face I couldn't tear my eyes away from. It seemed incongruous with the chaos of the fight—a beautiful teenager's face, relaxed and serene, with a small smile playing about her lips like you'd expect to see the lunch period after she'd aced a test. That same feeling of untouchability.

She pivoted inside Diamondback's guard and drove her elbow forward savagely into his chest. He stumbled back three paces, coughing, and Kira pressed her advantage . . .

And then she was thrown into the air by some countermove, turning too fast, slamming face-up into the concrete floor. Her head hit with a loud smack. My heart leaped right into my throat and stayed there, clogging it.

"Holy shit," whispered Z while I tried to swallow.

I wrenched my gaze away from the fight to look at him. His eyes and mouth were both wide open. I put a comforting hand on his shoulder, and to my surprise, he didn't knock it off, or glare, or make some snide comment. On the other hand, maybe he hadn't even noticed.

He sucked in a breath as the crowd gasped. They'd been a little quieter this fight than the last—there was probably something about watching a teenage girl in the ring sapping their enthusiasm. I turned back to the fight, but my hand stayed where it was.

Kira'd managed to rise in the few seconds I'd been looking away, but her nose bled freely—broken, maybe. She was moving oddly too, and I thought the headcrack might've disoriented her.

But her eyes were bright and clear, and she still wore that carefree smile, though it now looked kinda forced.

"Why ain't she tapping out?" asked Z. I wasn't sure if he was talking to me or himself, but it didn't matter because I didn't know. Though I did have one guess—she was having too much fun.

Diamondback stumbled, and Kira threw him over her hip. He managed to turn the tumble into a controlled roll, but Kira was already spinning after him. She dove as he came up and sent him sprawling back to the ground.

I could see her head wound clearly now, bleeding copiously down the back of her shirt. I had to reassure myself that head wounds bleed a lot, but it was *still* scary watching that much blood drain away. No wonder she was disoriented.

But she was angry. And perhaps the worst place you can be's beneath an angry Kira, woozy *or* alert. She straddled Diamondback's broad chest and rained blows down on him. He tried to flip over, but she shifted with him. He tried to block her blows, but she battered through his guard like he wasn't even there.

Much too late, he reached his meaty hands around her throat and squeezed, but by that point, it was basically over. Using both his hands for choking left his face open to even more abuse, and he didn't have the willpower left to withstand it. He let go, and Kira lifted his head and slammed it onto the ground, just like he'd done to her.

"That's it." Z nudged me, sounding relieved. He pointed at Diamondback's right arm, which he'd thrust skyward. "He's yielding."

But Kira grabbed the wrist and forced it down. There was shock among the crowd—they'd seen.

The whistle blew, but Kira didn't stop. She slammed

Diamondback's head onto the concrete again. She was doing it a third time when a bouncer caught her around the waist from behind and dragged her off.

Z was grayer than he'd been when Kira was *losing*.

"What the fuck," he managed at last.

"Your crush is psycho," is exactly what I *didn't* say. Even if I wanted to. Even if he probably already knew—especially after *that* display. So while I decided what to say, I looked at Kira in the ring, standing victorious over the moaning Diamondback, breathing hard and slowly relaxing as adrenaline drained from her body. She looked . . . *flushed*. Content.

But it was an eighteen-year-old middle-class teenager's contentment, and it didn't belong here, in an illegal fight club.

Yet as I saw how few spectators were approaching the betting counter, and remembered the fifteen-to-one odds on "Queen Bitch," I thought to myself—though I hated myself for thinking it—that we could—safely, of course, without putting her in any *real* danger—turn the situation to our advantage.

TEN

"No."

All my patience was going toward not cursing Kira out. Only the fear of another blow to the face held me back at this point. Part of me insisted that caving to violent threats wasn't a winning strategy, but my self-preservation instincts were happily dominant for now.

"Dammit Kira, I'm trying to forget you were there at all—against my orders, need I remind you—and work with you."

"No."

My mask must've cracked and let my irritation through, because Kira gave me a full blast of patented

Kira-contempt right out her eye-holes. "You pissed about that? You think you can tell me to not do shit and I'll stay in my time-out chair like a good little puppy?"

"Ignoring the mixed metaphor—" Addie sighed. "Okay, girl, look. Jason's kind of in charge. Since, like, *forever.* That doesn't mean he's more important—"

It did.

"—but it means when he gives an order, you listen. Even if it's leaving the last cookie in the cookie jar, and you know he's only saying that so he can eat it later when you aren't looking. Because having someone who can't be gainsaid is *important*, and if Jason can't rely on us to follow orders—"

Kira grinned wickedly. "Bet that attitude's fun in bed. Eh, Jace?"

I can count on one hand the times I've seen Addie speechless, and this was one of them. Her mouth opened like she was gonna start yelling and then just *hung* there—still open but frozen in place with shock.

"Yep, I'm sure it does," said Kira, undeterred by the lack of a response. "But I don't need the kid's plans anymore. I'll make my own, and they'll go wrong and peeps'll try and stop me, and I'll kick all their asses so hard they can't sit right in the *grave*."

It was . . . pretty hard to argue with that, actually, especially after what she'd done in the ring. She must've been outweighed three-to-one . . . and they'd pulled *her* off *him*.

Kira's hair was now washed and carefully covering whatever Diamondback'd done to her head, and I *really* wasn't gonna ask about it.

I breathed a deep lungful of air, made sure my voice was level. That was part of being the leader—not just giving orders the team could trust, but controlling your emotions, being the voice of certainty, of neutrality.

Kira couldn't see the slightest weakness from me, or she'd jump on it. And I was feeling *very* weak right now.

"There's gotta be some compromise you'd like," I said, spreading my palms in a placating gesture. "But if you just say 'no,' that makes it hard to figure out what part you don't like."

Kira shrugged. "All of it."

Deep breaths. Deep breaths.

"Let's start again," I tried. "So I say, 'Let's do a couple rigged matches to raise the cash to pay off the mob,' and you say . . ."

"No."

Deep breaths. The deepest fucking breaths ever. "Why not?"

"It's a stupid plan."

"What makes it stupid?" I was gonna poison Kira's mutton and I wouldn't even feel bad about it.

"Makes the fights too easy," said Kira. "There's no point if I know I'm gonna win. Why not just bet on me anyway? I'll win, you'll get your money, and we're both happy."

I caught Addie's eye and I could tell we'd amended Kira's sentence the exact same way—*unless I lose.*

"Now we're getting somewhere. Your primary objection to my proposal's a lack of challenge or randomness, and therefore, suspense. Correct?"

"Does that mean your plan's shit because whoever I'm beating doesn't have a chance of beating me back?"

"Yes."

"Then, yeah." Kira shrugged again.

I still couldn't tell if Kira's ignorant attitude was affected or genuine. My working assumption was a mix of both, cultivated to hide her legitimate shortcomings, but that theory had two issues. First, my model of Kira didn't give a shit if people thought she was dumb. Second, it didn't actually *tell* me which of her behaviors were fake and which were real.

But she'd been my friend long enough to understand that *last* sentence easily.

"Your odds won't stay high," said Z.

It was the first thing he'd said since, "Hey," when he'd arrived. He'd been unnaturally quiet since, which suited me fine, as he usually took Kira's side in arguments. I wondered what he'd made of her display in the warehouse, and whether it was contributing to his mood. Judging from how he wasn't meeting her eye even as he talked to her, it was likely a significant component.

"You're still a newcomer, so people ain't used to

you," Z explained. "But word's spreading pretty fast, and soon nobody's gonna bet against you. And then your odds'll go down *fast*—maybe even tip toward other guy."

Kira smirked. "Then maybe they'll gimme a tough fight. You boners better get your bets in quick if you wanna make some dosh before the ring catches on."

A tough fight . . .

The emaciated skeleton of an idea suggested itself, and I nourished it with attention. There's a whole psychology around getting people to do things, and one of my favorite methods is called the *foot in the door*. Basically, if someone agrees to something minor, it gets them in a frame of mind to agree to bigger things later. In theory, if I found *something* Kira'd cooperate with, she'd more readily cooperate again in the future.

In theory. If you put the world's leading psychologists in a room with Kira, I think their heads'd explode from frustration.

But hey, worth a shot. Step one, *find a compromise*.

"Thanks for the analysis, Z," I said, which I'd meant

genuinely but somehow made sound sarcastic. "Tell me this, do they ever do matches with special rules? Like, one guy has to survive against six for a full minute, one guy gets a baseball bat but has an arm tied behind his back, stuff like that."

Z considered. "It's been done. Well, not like *that*, but same idea. It's by mutual agreement."

"And the parameters of these matches would drastically affect the odds, yeah?"

"Course. You wanna set something up?"

"Maybe." This next part had to be phrased delicately, because I only had one shot. "I have an idea. A compromise."

Kira opened her mouth to object and I quickly corrected myself, chastising myself internally for not catching that mistake. "Not even a compromise, really. Kira gets what she wants, we get what we want. All of it."

"Win-win," I added when nobody spoke up to say how great that sounded.

The others continued to cede the floor, so I

reluctantly kept speaking. "How does that work? What a great question, I was just getting to that. Kira wants a fair, risky fight. We want five million dollars for the *save Z's ass* fund. Here's what I propose. Kira volunteers to do this crazy special fight. Like, her hands're tied behind her back, or she only has thirty seconds to knock her opponent out, or every time she throws a punch she can't throw another until she takes a hit. Something that drives the odds sky-high. Then we rig the fight *just a little*—not enough to ruin the challenge, just enough to make it doable. Since the odds'll be so high, we won't have to risk as much to make a fortune. If Kira loses, we can just bet again."

None of that plan addressed my *real* motivation, which was to keep Kira from being seriously injured, but I didn't see a way around that risk given her attitude. Sometimes, your best isn't good enough. (Not that making a reasoned argument *was* my best—If I *really* needed to stop Kira at the expense of all other goals, I'd just tell Derek's team to hold her family hostage. But I wasn't *that* desperate. Yet.)

Kira screwed up her face in thought . . . but slowly, it relaxed into a smile. "I kinda like it. As long as whatever I'm doing's super badass. Like fighting a dragon, only actually possible."

Z and Addie were looking skeptical. I didn't wanna acknowledge them in case Kira noticed, but I tried to give off *trust-me* vibes. Hopefully they got the message.

"And like, it'd add to Queen Bitch's mystique, right?" mused Kira. "She took on impossible odds and kicked their ass. What'll she do to *you*?"

"Kick their ass, probably," I said as deadpan as I could, but Kira didn't even notice.

"Yup."

It was then that Z requested a word in private.

"Sure," I said, not looking at Addie in case she had a pleading *take me too* look—which I unfortunately couldn't do, or Kira'd *know* something was up.

Luckily, I had experience with private conversations in Kira's house—a couple more and I'd be a grizzled veteran. The Applewoods' guest bedroom'd worked when I'd needed to talk to Addie, so I led Z there.

"What's up?" I asked, after I'd shut and locked the door.

He didn't meet my eye, or respond.

"Dude, you're kinda scaring me today." Maybe our relationship was rocky right now, but now could be an opportunity to reverse some of the damage.

"What's up with Kira?"

There was a question that could take several hours to answer fully. "She's not okay," I said truthfully.

"Yeah, now tell me something that isn't *fucking obvious.*" Z rounded on the wall and punched it as hard as he could, then grimaced in pain. "Ow, shit. *Shit.*"

It was the same reaction he'd had back in the Bronx, when he'd kicked the telephone pole. "You should really stop doing that," I said, knowing he wouldn't listen.

He'd left an impression in the wood—a series of pockmarks where his knuckles'd impacted. Now he was cradling his right hand in his other, massaging it experimentally and wincing. I sank down onto the bed, wondering when my friends'd met up without me and decided to go nuts.

"I *know* what's up," he finally said, as much to the air as me. "Goddammit, I've known since DC. I've been pretending like I don't. I ain't proud of that. I wanted to make you say it so I could pretend I was hearing it for the first time, but fuck it, you don't gotta—I know."

"I won't pretend otherwise," I said hollowly, and Z's head snapped up at the sound, finally looking at me. I could see every burden the last six months'd placed on him clearly in his prematurely-lined face.

"Then why're you encouraging her?"

"Because there's nothing else I *can* do," I admitted. "She's *this* close to walking out as is, and if she does, I can't do *anything* for her. She's in a real bad place, and when I figure out how to help her out of it, I will."

Z's voice was flat and hard. "You're supposed to be best friends."

I remembered the feeling of Kira's fist striking my cheek, the firmness of the floor as I fell against it. "Supposed to be."

There was a bitter stinging feeling behind my eyes, an almost-familiar sensation, but one I couldn't place.

It was only when I felt the tear tickling my skin that I realized my eyes were wet.

Thankfully, Z pretended not to notice as I wiped it away.

"That ring's dangerous," he said. "They don't play fair. If Kira wins too much, they'll stack the deck. You saw her head—a couple more hits like that and she'll be in the hospital. Fuck, she should be there *now*. Why the fuck're you letting her do this?"

I gave a small but triumphant smile. "You mean the plan I shared back there?"

"If she gets hurt because you—"

"She won't," I said. "I don't care what I told Kira, I'm gonna throw whatever match we arrange like it's on fire, until the only way she can lose is if she trips over her own feet."

As far as I was concerned, this meeting was over. I got up off the bed and clapped Z on the shoulder. "She won't be in any danger, I promise—not one bit."

ELEVEN

THE RESTAURANT'S CLOCK SAID *7:01*, BUT MY PHONE displayed a more accurate *6:58*. No need for search parties yet . . . but I was anxious. Dates always did that to me—even after dozens of successes, my brain remained fully convinced things were seconds away from going suddenly, drastically wrong.

But nothing *had* gone wrong, nothing *would* go wrong, there was no *reason* for things to go wrong. Unlike almost all our other dinners, this was no carefully-plotted prelude to a confidence scheme, or even a chance to meet and discuss sensitive matters away from the others. It was just a dinner date, fancy-dress, stressors and business checked at the door in favor of small talk and risk-free flirting. Like normal couples.

But sitting in the atrium, picking at nonexistent loose threads, watching my phone's clock transition smoothly to read *6:59*, wondering if something urgent'd come up on Addie's end . . . well, the never-ending parade of pressing business was almost—*almost*—preferable.

She arrived at exactly seven, of course, fetching as always in a cream blouse, black hair just barely peeking past her chin. She saw me immediately and one of her patented small-but-genuine smiles, the infectious kind, eased over her face.

"You made it," I said, and my relief must've shown, because she rolled her eyes.

"I won't even ask if I'm late, because I happen to know I'm not."

But there was playfulness in her exasperation, and affection in that thin-lipped smile.

She took my hands and we kissed lightly. It still

surprised me, sometimes, how right it felt. *This.* I should do this more often.

. . . Well, probably not *much* more often, or my to-do list'd grow faster than an outmatched hydra. But I could *probably* justify a few more breaks.

We had reservations, so we didn't have to wait—a table was set for us by a wide-paneled window overlooking New York City's skyline from the forty-third story. The sun was only just dipping toward the horizon—if we ate slowly enough, we could watch the sunset all the way down. I was lost for a few seconds in the view, but our waiter, who probably looked through that window several dozen times a day, didn't spare it a second glance as he filled our drinks and departed, leaving two menus behind.

Addie's eyes widened as she opened one.

"It's cute how you still do that every time I take you out," I grinned.

"It's always so damn *expensive*," said Addie, staring at the entree section like it was printed on baby skin.

"Expense is a relative matter," I said sagely. "If you can afford quality, do so."

I didn't mention where I'd heard that particular chestnut—from Lucas Jorgensen, across a white linen tablecloth much like this one.

Nor did I recite his words in full, which continued as follows—"I'm giving you a taste for quality while I can, before you get set in your ways. That way, you'll have to pick a vocation that can support this lifestyle. No becoming an actor for you, boy—that's a life of canned beans and peanut butter. That sound good? Better than tenderloin steak, cooked rare while you wait?"

Well, it'd *worked* . . . although my chosen career involved more acting than Lucas might've approved of.

One fake ID later and I was sipping a Riesling pensively, making small chat about Addie's cousins.

" . . . Like when we were seven, maybe six, at the park. And we were playing hide-and-seek, just us, as kids do."

I *mmm*ed politely, flipping idly through the menu. "I remember being super tired for some reason. Maybe I had lots of homework the night before, or . . . well, not important. Long story short, I fell asleep waiting for her to find me. When I woke up, it was dark out and a cop was shaking me awake."

I laughed. "Must've been a good spot."

"Yeah, that's what I thought. But I could never use it again because that event was burnt into everyone's memories, so they always looked there first. So I found others." Addie's smile widened a few notches. "Anyway, they aren't leaving for another few days and they want to meet you, so you should come by before they go."

"I'll try to pencil it in somewhere amidst the madness."

"Right," said Addie sympathetically. "How was your day?"

"Pretty good," I said. "Let's see, I met with Diesel—you know, the guy Kira's gonna fight. He was real understanding about—"

"Vacation!" said Addie quickly, pointing at my mouth with an admonishing finger. "No business allowed!"

She was right, of course. And while I'd realized leaving work at the door might be hard—hence the code word *vacation* we'd set up in advance as a quick warning—I hadn't expected to fuck up that quickly.

"Fair." I grinned ruefully. "But one last thing on that, I couldn't figure out if the guy's a fan of trains or *West Side Story*."

"Oh, you've seen *West Side Story?*"

I had. Lucas'd used it as an opportunity to highlight the perils of poor communication.

The conversation that sprang up from there lasted a solid fifteen minutes, until appetizers arrived. Keeping business and leisure separate was *easy*.

Over appetizers, discussion shifted to gossip about absent friends—not being here to defend themselves, they were easy targets.

"Z's still striking out so far," Addie reported. "Poor guy."

"I dunno if 'striking out' is the right phrase anymore," I said. "You weren't at the fight, but *we* were. And don't take this the wrong way, but if I saw *you* take someone apart like that, with a goofy grin that big—yeah, it looked just like how you're imagining—I dunno if I could . . . "

"No," said Addie at last, staring fixedly at her water. "I get it."

"So she might've finally scared him off. He's got a good heart, he won't wanna . . . Oh man. Shit. If Z stops going after Kira, what's keeping him around? Not my company—I've been trying to smooth things over, but—"

"Vacation," said Addie firmly. "We can discuss how to keep the CPC together later. What I'm worried about is Kira. She's always been a bit crazy, but—"

"Vacation. Important, but vacation."

"No way, that's—"

"Uh-huh—"

"— Just concern for a friend."

"It is a current source of *severe* stress," I said, letting some of that inner ache into my voice. "Can we skip it for now? Please?"

"Fair enough," conceded Addie. "Well . . . "

I waited.

The silence stretched on.

I kept waiting.

Then I started to laugh, in spite of myself. Addie looked at me strangely, and while I couldn't read her face, I knew she was relieved to have an excuse to talk.

"What?"

I just laughed harder, which was weird, because it wasn't even funny. "We're *really* bad at talking about normal people stuff."

That got another smile out of Addie. "Yeah. I guess that's sad, or whatever."

"A little." I cast about for something, anything to talk about. There was the Mafia, our rogue teammate, all sorts of plans (some little, some of vital importance) . . . Well, none of *those* would do.

"Steal anything cool lately?" I tried at last.

"That's another 'vacation,' actually," said Addie. "Nice try, though."

Back to silence.

"I don't suppose you've got anything to talk about?"

Addie tapped her knife against the table, making a dull thudding noise on the linen. "I can be really bad at this kind of thing."

We were interrupted by dinner—lamb over potatoes with a side of grilled zucchini for me, and avgolemono soup with stuffed peppers for Addie. Grateful for the reprieve, I dug in. The lamb was acceptable, if slightly overdone, but the potatoes were worthy of consideration as high art—crispy on the outside, soft on the inside, and seasoned to perfection with a light dusting of salt and rosemary.

"I think we're focusing on the wrong thing," said Addie, looking up from her meal. Her peppers, cut into small pieces carefully calculated to just below bite-size, lay scattered on her plate. "With the money. Money's always been easy to—"

"Vacation," I warned again around a mouthful of potato.

Addie looked at me wryly. "Can we give up on that? It obviously didn't work, and there's lots of important stuff to discuss. As long as we're both here."

I felt a small, rebellious tingle of relief.

"Yeah," I said. "It was a dumb idea anyway. I just thought . . ."

But the words caught coming up, and I couldn't articulate *what* I'd thought. It made me wanna start laughing again. Then suddenly I *was*, and Addie's hands were on my shoulders, head next to mine, and I realized I wasn't laughing at all, I was crying bitterly (which I *never* do) for the *second* time this week, and I didn't even know *why*. Maybe for the relationship we could've had, if we were normal. But why shed tears over that? It was a hypothetical. It'd never existed. You don't cry over something that never existed. Besides, people were probably staring.

So I stopped.

"I'm fine," I said when I trusted myself to speak. "Really."

Addie didn't look convinced—which was smart of her, as I hadn't even convinced myself. "Babe . . . "

"It's really nothing," I said, taking one of her hands. "I just . . . thought we could leave it all behind for a night, you know?"

"So did I," said Addie quietly. "We tried."

"I think we did okay until now."

"Yeah." Addie brought the edge of the tablecloth to my eyes and dabbed expertly. The part of me that remembered Lucas's lessons cried out at the breach of restaurant etiquette, but as it was Addie, I let it pass.

Now I could *definitely* feel the stares. And if *I* could, it must've been like the heat of an open flame to Addie. But she gave no sign of noticing, intent as she was on her task.

That's when I knew her fears were groundless. Lucas could *never've* put aside a room's opinion of him for something as trivial as a man in tears.

And when she was done, she didn't mock my

weakness like *he* would've. She just dropped the tablecloth and slipped back into her seat across from me, all composed professionalism.

"So," I said, moving past that embarrassing moment as best I could. "We failed. This is why you don't date coworkers."

I'd meant it as a joke, and Addie took it as one. "Are we really coworkers, though? I'd say *conspirators* is more accurate."

"This is why you don't date conspirators."

"Nobody says that."

"Fair enough." I hesitated. Talking about business still felt like defeat. "I rigged the match."

"I gathered," said Addie. "I'm more worried about the Mafia's deal. Cash for Z's life, and probably ours. Only we know from Vegas, they don't always honor their deals as well as their code suggests."

"Richard made it look like we'd betrayed them that time," I deflected. I'd thought about this very subject quite a bit. "We dunno if there's anything to fear from Lorenzo—"

"—Exactly," said Addie. "We don't know. So we don't assume. Maybe we raise the money and they bump Z off anyway. Maybe they get the rest of us too—we've been annoying enough. If I were them, I wouldn't let us live."

I should've known she'd be too smart to keep in the dark. Course, she wouldn't be the same girl I'd fallen for if she wasn't.

"Yeah, neither would I. Odds are, they've got something extra in mind for us," I conceded. "But I have *several* extra somethings in mind for them . . ."

TWELVE

I HADN'T NOTICED THE CASH BAR ACROSS THE WAREHOUSE from the betting counter last time, which just goes to show that even the best of us can make mistakes.

I'd had a fake ready, but they didn't even check ID. Still, it was nice knowing nobody here *cared* whether a teenager ordered a White Russian, especially when those White Russians were made with half-and-half instead of milk—an incredible innovation that'll take hold across America if I get my way.

Tell your friends.

I wasn't used to drinking while standing, but I couldn't leave my front-row seat or I'd lose it to another patron eager to drink in the coming spectacle—Queen Bitch (Kira Applewood to her friends) versus a mystery opponent in a special high-stakes match. Peter Storm's hype-men were really amping the drama. Kira, now on something of a winning streak, had a small-but-loyal cult following, and this match'd been built up as the one that might finally bring the Queen of the Ring down into the dirt.

Maybe literally, given the handicap—Kira'd be fighting with fifteen-pound weights strapped to each arm, and another thirty around her neck. She'd be slower and tire faster. If we hadn't paid Diesel twenty thousand dollars to lose convincingly, I would've doubted her ability to win . . . and therefore would never've let the match go forward at all. But if she'd known Diesel was gonna throw it, she'd have refused to fight on principle, so I was hoping that'd stay a secret forever.

For the average patron, though, the details were a mystery. The nature of the handicap, the opponent, even the odds—all would be unknown until ten minutes before the fight, at which point the combatants'd enter the arena and last-minute betting, with proper odds, would open up.

It was T-minus twelve now, and Z was in position by the betting counter—we'd be using the official bookies. We needed reliability. If a private bettor decided disappearing was cheaper than paying us, we'd be helpless—and with the amount we were looking to win, that was a very real concern. Kira's teenage-girl look wasn't fooling people anymore, but the handicap would hopefully keep the odds high. Six-to-one was my estimate.

I'd invested in a set of fake nails for Kira—the method by which she'd be ostensibly winning the match. They were practically invisible, but sharper than most knives and coated with a fast-acting mild sedative. I'd been assured by my sources (which will remain nameless as per our ongoing agreement) that this was top-level equipment, and the price tag certainly backed that assertion. Of course, Kira wouldn't need them, but *she* couldn't know that.

I drained and crumpled the plastic cup, then considered. If I looked for a trashcan, I'd forfeit my hard-won place, but I wasn't gonna hold my trash like an idiot while watching Diesel job to one of my former best friends.

"Hey," I beckoned at a stranger behind me. He eyed me suspiciously through thick lashes. I didn't blame him—*everyone* here was suspicious in some way.

Slowly, making sure he could follow my every move, I extracted a twenty from my wallet, which I folded and dropped into the cup.

"You mind tossing this for me?"

He didn't mind one bit.

Now happily unencumbered, I turned back to the empty-yet-illuminated ring, already toasting another successful scheme with the gang . . . until the realization that I could really only call one of them "friend" anymore left a sudden, unwelcome weight in my chest.

How far had we fallen? How far did we have left to fall?

I forced myself off that train of thought.

The speaker system cut in with a high-pitched whine. "Ladies and gentlemen," the voice said from the booth. "This is it. The moment you've been waiting for. Please give a warm welcome to . . . Queen Bitch!"

The crowd went crazy. She hadn't been fighting a week and they loved her already, their beautiful, unlikely, undefeated champion. She stopped just inside the illuminated circle and gave the crowd a fierce grin.

Her eyes landed on me, and stopped there.

She *winked*.

Something caught in the recesses of my brain, a snag, something wasn't right . . .

Kira's arms swung loose, unencumbered. Weight-free. Actually, I couldn't see *anything* that could be construed as a handicap, aside from a mottling of bruises around her neck and a long gash along her scalp, partially hidden by her tightly-braided hair.

Every meeting, she showed up with new injuries—I wondered what her parents thought.

"Veeery nice," said the speakers. It was tough identifying any discernible emotion through the distortion, but the voice sounded somewhat amused. "Now give it up for her opponents!"

The man who entered the ring was *not* Diesel. He was shorter, swarthier, with a shock of dark hair, a bristly black mustache, and an open, predatory stance.

Before I could even begin wondering what was going on, I realized they'd said "opponent*s.*"

And Diesel stepped into the ring.

My poor brain generated potential explanations, extrapolated their probabilities, and spit out the relieving notion that as Diesel *was* still involved, Kira's odds were still pretty good, especially with the nails in the mix. I was so wrapped up in my thoughts, I almost missed the *third* man, on the heels of the first two.

He was big—that's the first thing I noticed. A wild giant, coarsely stubbled with brown bristles. Palms like dinner plates. Teeth like thimbles. Eyes like a shark's, dark and cold.

I gasped. And I wasn't the only one. There was a veritable *chorus* of whispers around the circle, amidst wide applause.

"I give you The Admiral, Diesel, and Troglodyte," said the speakers, and again, there was that flurry of discomfort. Or maybe I was just imagining things—I was, after all, discomforted enough for everyone here. *Two* extra opponents? What the hell'd happened?

Whatever it was, Kira didn't seemed concerned. There was a triumphant grin on her face, and she was tapping her foot impatiently. She stared down the giant like she could barely resist charging him then and there. Meanwhile, I was scared for myself just *looking* at the guy. If someone said I had to fight him tomorrow, I'd take the next train out of town.

"Queen Bitch will face all three opponents, one right after the other, until she's defeated. Fights are to surrender, other than the last, which is to uncon- sciousness. How many opponents can Queen Bitch make it through? The betting counter's open for the next ten minutes, so place your bets now."

The voice cut out melodramatically, and there were suddenly far fewer people standing around me and a very long line at the betting counter . . . which Z would already be at the front of. His five-hundred thousand dollar budget represented a quarter of our current total assets. With six-to-one odds, we'd have been about halfway to our goal after accounting for Diesel's bribe . . . but this was a completely different match. The odds could be *anything*.

"Kira," I said, trying to pitch my voice so only she'd hear me. "Kira, do you know what's happening?"

She ignored me. Or didn't hear. Whatever.

There was a small choking noise behind me and I turned to see Z staring wide-eyed at Troglodyte. "Big," he managed at last, then staggered over on unsteady legs, not taking his eyes off Kira's most intimidating opponent.

"Big," I agreed. "What odds did we get?"

Z took a deep breath to recover himself. "Forget

that, what the hell is this? If you changed the plan without saying—"

"No, I'm as surprised as you. At least she isn't weighed down."

"I fucked up," said Z, still looking aghast. "Dude, this is bad. They had different odds depending on how many fights you thought Kira could win. I bet on her beating all three. But that was before I saw *him*. I should've bet lower, I should've—"

"The *odds*, dude."

"Fourteen-to-one against," said Z. "Six-to-one against for her beating two. Seven million greenbacks, I . . . This one bet would've done it. I couldn't say no. Figured you had some new plan—"

"I just wish I knew what happened," I said, realizing as I said so that it was patently *obvious* what'd happened—I was deluding myself if I thought otherwise. The smile on Kira's face as she sized up her opponents made it crystal clear.

She must've known I'd do more than slip her some sedative-laced fingernails. Because that was what I *did*—head off failure at *every* point of risk. Of *course* I'd have brought Diesel aboard.

So Kira'd gone behind my back and set up a match for herself, one where the risk was real. And while the lighting was too dim to tell, I suspected she wasn't wearing the nails either.

How very like her. Which is to say, *utterly infuriating*.

Not all was lost, not yet. If Kira could take The Admiral, she had, at least theoretically, a free win against Diesel—I'd certainly paid him enough. That left Troglodyte.

"You know anything about Troglodyte?" I asked casually.

Z blanched. "That's *Troglodyte*?"

Shit. Shit, shit, *shit*.

"Didn't you hear them say—?"

"It was loud over there and the speakers sucked," said Z. "If I'd heard *Troglodyte*, I . . . Oh, man."

His expression was one of abject horror. And was that *sweat* on his brow?

"You know how I said things were bad? Well, this is *really* bad. Mondo bad. We gotta stop the match."

His panic was almost enough to break me out of my need for precise information and just *act*. But that need was part of who I was, and not easily discarded.

"Talk. Who is this guy?"

Z spoke rapidly, trying to cram everything into as short an explanation as possible. He knew if I asked a question, I'd need the answer to make any plan at all. "Undefeated, super popular years back. Brutal. Barred from the ring when he *killed* his opponent—"

What.

"—The ring cut ties. Even then, the homicide investigation almost brought everything down. Figured he was in jail, he should be, he . . . "

I twisted the dial on the part of my brain responsible for picking up the sounds Z was making to *off*.

Two things were clear.

First—If *I* were in charge, there's just *one* reason I'd bring a killer back to fight. The obvious one.

Second, related to the first—we had to stop this match. Right now.

"New question," I said, cutting Z off mid-sentence. "What're the protocols for canceling a match?"

Z shook his head slowly. "There ain't any."

The air was solidifying in my lungs, becoming harder and harder to breathe . . .

But *any* problem's solvable given enough time. So shut down distractions, examine problem's parameters and available resources . . .

A loud whistle interrupted my reverie.

"Time's up," said Z. "What've you got?"

I didn't have anything.

THIRTEEN

STEPPED FORWARD.

I couldn't think of anything else to do, but *any-thing* was better than doing nothing.

There was a sharp tug on my collar and I stumbled back.

"You dumbass," hissed Z. "You know what they'd do to you?"

I didn't. And while I rankled at being called a dumbass (especially by *Z*, of all people), I was willing to concede he knew this place better. Besides, it was *his* crush in the ring—if he thought my trying to save her was a bad idea, it was probably a *really* bad idea.

Kira and The Admiral were circling just out of

arm's reach of each other. Diesel and Troglodyte'd retreated into the shadows.

"We gotta do something," I said calmly. "Troglodyte being here's *not* a coincidence. They want—"

Z just stared at me, looking tormented. He knew.

"You've got two fights' time to solve this," he said. "And if you say you can't, I'm out, I don't care—"

"Well, it's hard when I dunno how this place works. Why don't you explain things more?"

Kira darted forward, legs snapping into position like the world's fastest pair of shears. She'd smelled weakness.

The Admiral wisely chose to step back rather than meet the charge, dropped down on one hand, and swung his legs out, attempting to trip her. But she leaped over the kick, and only a last-second roll kept her heels from coming down on his chest.

It was only a minor delay, and both fighters knew it. Kira dove onto the prone Admiral and, after a minor scuffle, had him pinned.

"Give up," Kira growled, her voice carrying

through the building. She punctuated her request with a knee to the chest.

Management must've given Kira a talking-to about sportsmanship and acceptable behavior after Diamondback. Or maybe the fight'd been over before she could lose control . . .

"I can just . . . " A grunt of exertion as The Admiral tried another escape maneuver and failed. He was rewarded with an open-palmed slap to the temple. " . . . Keep hurting you 'til you give. So *do it*."

She pitched as The Admiral writhed beneath her, but recovered and waited until he sagged, hopeless. "I yield," he said, and Kira freed one of his arms so he could lift it in surrender. The whistle blew, short and conclusive, and Kira stood, eyes blazing with triumph.

The crowd loved it. The speed, the style . . . a brilliant example of Queen Bitch's technique—or so the enthusiastic conversations around me opined.

I clapped earnestly with the rest—happy, at least,

that Kira'd managed to win quickly, without any injuries, preserving energy.

But I'd kinda needed a *longer* fight, because I still had no ideas and if Diesel threw in the towel early, it'd be Kira versus at least two hundred fifty pounds of muscle and rage. *Murderous* rage.

There was a second whistle, and Diesel entered the illuminated circle. He didn't even glance at me—which didn't necessarily mean anything, ours was a discreet arrangement, but seeing as everything else'd gone wrong, I wouldn't be surprised if he'd decided to take the money and fight to win anyway. Or someone else'd bribed him the other way. Or something.

If so, I *would* come after him. If you let someone get away with that even once, *everyone* starts doing it.

Kira raised her hands into a boxing stance and waded in.

Diesel was good—much better than The Admiral. Several times, he landed a blow that doubled her over in pain. But each time, rather than follow up his advantage, he backed off and let her recover.

It looked mocking, an illusion enhanced by the confident grin he gave the crowd every time he did it. But I knew the real reason, and I was grateful at least *something* was working as intended.

Still, couldn't he just *lose*?

Kira stood, breathing hard, at the far edge of the ring. There was a thick sheen of sweat on her forehead. Her tank top was soaked through, and stained with blood where a tear in her ear'd leaked down her neck onto it. Diesel was still going strong, which I took as confirmation Kira'd ditched the nails. So much for fast-acting sedatives. Did I mention I was gonna kill her?

"Finish her!" someone yelled, finally fed up with Diesel's cocky asshole act. There were some answering shouts of agreement.

Diesel turned indulgently toward the crowd, raising a good-natured hand as if saying *be patient, we'll get there.* In that moment, Kira struck, bounding across the gap between them with all she had.

The crowd surged and gasped and gave Diesel all the warning he needed to turn around. But perhaps because of their goading, he stepped forward and met the assault head-on. And that was his mistake.

Kira battered him mercilessly, not giving him the chance to mount a counterattack. He managed a half-hearted jab at her abdomen, but she took the blow with a grunt and responded with a windmill punch against Diesel's jaw. Something crunched. Diesel stumbled back a half-step.

Faster than my eyes could register, Kira leveraged his temporary weakness into a high kick to his upper chest, just below the neck. He fell and, before Kira could follow up, lifted his arm.

Kira reluctantly stepped back and allowed her opponent to limp away. The smile was back on her face, but it looked more like a grimace. She shook her head like she was trying to clear it.

"*Jason,*" murmured Z.

And there it was, in my head. A plan.

I had three private security teams at my disposal. They were being paid to guard, not raid, but they'd follow my orders as long as I signed the checks. Diverting a team *here*, staging a stick-up of some kind . . . would've been a great idea ten minutes ago, but by now it was far too late. The closest team'd probably take twenty minutes to arrive . . . and I'd be surprised if Kira lasted five against Troglodyte. Not even the nails would've made it close to a fair fight.

Even so, might as well try. I pulled out my cellphone and started typing.

The whistle blew a third time.

"I've got something," I said in a voice I hoped sounded reassuring. "It might not work, but I'm giving it a shot."

Which meant, of course, *it's not gonna work, but you can't say I did nothing if Kira—*

But I couldn't bring myself to think it.

The fighters closed, and almost immediately, Troglodyte sank a fist into Kira's head. She didn't so much as stumble—but seconds later, she took another identical blow and swayed a little.

She disengaged, took a couple steps back. The crowd was hushed, straining their eyes to take in every second of this fight.

"Christ, but you're a *fast* motherfucker," said Kira. "You're too big to be that fast."

She spat and ground it in with her heel.

Troglodyte just smiled. It didn't suit his face.

He stepped forward and Kira danced back. She'd learned from that first disastrous exchange, and she was conceding the contest of raw power, opting instead to out-maneuver him. The only problem was, Kira's biggest advantage'd never been her maneuverability.

It was her raw power.

Still, a defensive strategy seemed to serve her well as she circled Troglodyte like an orbiting satellite, jabbing in whenever she saw an opening. Finally, Troglodyte responded with a relatively sluggish and telegraphed haymaker, which Kira anticipated, ducked under, and punished with a spinning kick to the chest like the one that'd floored Diesel.

Troglodyte blinked.

One massive hand shot out as Kira completed her spin, grabbing at her trailing braid. His fingers closed around it, and he *pulled*.

Kira flew past his right hip with a cry of surprise and pain. She hit the floor face-first and immediately rolled over, bracing for Troglodyte's next move. As he rushed her prone body, she wrapped her legs around him and squeezed.

He lifted her by the calves, pulled her in against him, and, as she scrambled for a stable position, got in three blows to her left side.

Then he ripped away her hold, turned her over, and threw her at the ground.

Z made a small choking noise, and I realized I hadn't been breathing.

Kira rolled and sprang to her feet ahead of Troglodyte's follow-up. She was bleeding freely from the forehead and nose—maybe the mouth too, but I couldn't tell. She shook her head again and dabbed at her face, assessing the damage.

And she was still smiling.

That, more than anything, made Troglodyte pause. Even through the blood, her smile shone clear as day—predatory, almost lascivious. Like she didn't notice her body slowly giving out.

And it *was*. She was worn out and hurt from Diesel, and feeling the pain of a couple dozen injuries from past fights. You could read how hard she was battling her brain's urge to shut down, and I wasn't sure how much longer she could possibly succeed. This was Kira's limit. There were no final reserves of strength, no last-minute surges of determination. Whatever she had left to bring, she had with her now. And it just wasn't enough.

Troglodyte approached at an easy pace, swinging out with his superior reach, forcing Kira back into the darker rim of the arena up against the crowd. They shuffled back, outside his range, away from the bloodied angel he fought.

To unconsciousness. Not to yield.

And it was *obvious* why they'd drawn the rules that way. They'd known Kira could beat the first two all along. A fighter like her didn't yield until she had no other choice—sometimes, not even then. And that choice would come in the third round if ever . . . so they'd removed it.

She'd been set up to fail from the start.

And as I realized this, she stumbled—her left leg gave way, toppling her onto the stone.

Troglodyte dove—it was too tempting an opening. But Kira recovered herself (so quickly I realized the initial stumble must've been deliberate) and threw herself at his legs as he came down. And then she was on his chest, punching down at his bare head, and then they were rolling in a tangle of limbs, striking every which way too quickly to follow . . .

Troglodyte emerged on top and brought his knee down into Kira's gut. He followed it up with jab after jab into her defenseless face.

Z turned away, but I watched in spite of myself,

unblinking, though looking became harder every second. Observing changed nothing, and it was better to know than to not know.

At last, satisfied, he stood. Stepped over Kira's body. Raised an arm in victory. There was some applause, but no cheering. Not after the sheer brutality of that last assault.

And then even that applause died out, giving way to awed gasps.

Kira was moving.

Not quickly, but she didn't have to be to qualify as conscious. Her face was a mess of bruises and open wounds, and there was swelling around one eye. But she stood defiantly, and her mouth twisted into something that could've been a grin.

Troglodyte looked at her in disbelief . . . and some measure of respect. "Should'a stayed down," he growled. And that was the truest thing I'd ever heard—my brain was generating a list of synonyms for *idiot*, all by Kira's name.

She said something in response, but it was too slurred to be understood.

Troglodyte shook his head and stepped forward, fists up.

And the chanting began. A murmur at first, but steadily rising in volume. "Queen Bitch, Queen Bitch, Queen Bitch . . ."

They closed one last time, without preamble. Kira defended his first couple swings more by luck than anything—I wasn't sure she could even *see* by now. And then she juked sideways, avoided his next swing, and stepped inside his guard.

His arms snapped shut like a bear trap around her, pinning her arms, and he began to squeeze.

She kicked at his legs, weaker and weaker as she gasped for air . . . And the chant fell silent as her struggles grew feebler still and her eyelids started fluttering . . . And I knew he wouldn't stop after she fell unconscious, or maybe Kira was built differently somehow and simply *didn't* fall unconscious, but either way, this was it, this was the end of the line, and no matter how tough things'd gotten recently, we'd been *friends*, and there were still a thousand things I needed to say—

Kira slumped in his arms.

"He's gonna kill her!" I shouted, hating how high and panicky my voice'd become. "Just like last time!"

It was all I could think to do, hope against hope that the crowd could be swayed to my side, that together, we could do *something* to stop him . . .

The crowd rumbled their support. Troglodyte looked up at me, eyes full of anger—and in that moment of distraction, Kira jerked forward, breaking his grip with a sudden surge of might, and sank her teeth into his neck.

Blood, flying through the air in spurts . . .

Up came her arm in a perfect arc, thumb outstretched, suddenly free from Troglodyte's grip as he put his hands to his neck, trying to stem the flow of blood.

I saw it coming a second before it happened, gritted my teeth, and *still* flinched back in horror as

Kira dug her thumb into Troglodyte's eye. It came out red to the knucklebone.

Troglodyte sank to his knees, roaring in agony and anger and helplessness. But his roars grew ever weaker as the blood forced its way between his fingers, and then they came not at all.

"I win," Kira croaked, and then collapsed.

Like a spell'd been broken, the crowd surged forward, running to Troglodyte's side, to Kira's side, checking vitals, shouting for first aid, for an ambulance, for *anything*—

"She's with us," I heard my mouth saying, and I realized my legs'd taken me to where Kira lay, breathing shallowly. "We'll take care of her."

I don't think anyone believed us. But none of them really wanted to stop us either. We lifted Kira between us in a two-man fireman's carry and shuffled toward the door.

"She parks in a lot a block down," said Z. I dunno how he knew, but I was glad he did.

"Her keys," I realized, mention of the car jogging my memory. "She won't have them on her—"

Z looked at me with wide, frightened eyes. No, not at me . . . *past* me. I heard the familiar *click* of a cocked weapon.

"Not another step."

I froze.

"Good. Put her down."

I did.

"Now turn around—you too, white guy."

I turned.

Two large-figured men in plainclothes had weapons trained on me.

"She needs a hospital," I said, trying to keep breathing. A circulatory system can only be expected to take so much.

"We've got a medical team on-site," said one of the men. "But she's not going nowhere."

His tone brooked no argument, and I figured it'd be a bad idea to point out the double negative. I closed my eyes momentarily, frustrated. "Get someone over here."

One of the men holstered his gun and started toward the crowd at a run. The other relieved us of our phones, just to make sure we couldn't get help from outside. Other staffers were shaking down patrons all over the warehouse—sealing the area down tight until further notice. Z wasn't too happy about it, but I didn't argue as much as I could've. I mostly just wanted this musclehead out of my face. Finally satisfied, he warned us sternly to stay put and wandered off toward another group of spectators.

"Well, long as we're sticking around, might as well collect our winnings."

Z nodded dumbly. "Winnings. Right."

As if tranced, he wandered back toward the betting counter.

He was only gone three minutes, but by the time he'd returned, Kira was surrounded by medical staff, all yelling urgent-sounding orders to each other. He locked eyes with me and shook his head.

"The fuck does that mean?"

"They won't pay."

Breathe, I reminded myself. "Why not?"

"Kira queered the match," said Z hollowly. "Troglodyte's dead."

If he said something else, I didn't hear it. There was a rushing in my ears, a dawning horror that someone else'd died as a result of my plans . . .

"Bullshit," I said, because I couldn't articulate my other feelings. "She won."

Z snorted in contempt—though whether at me or the rules, I couldn't tell. "All bets're null if someone dies."

We stood watching Kira's motionless body, trying to decipher the endless stream of medical jargon. It helped distract from what we'd seen her do.

A thirty-foot spray of blood, a red thumb pulling itself free from a socket . . .

"They'll keep her here, turn her in," said Z quietly. "Concoct some backstory for what happened. Make sure the police're happy. There's no way she'll avoid prison."

"Just what I needed," I said dryly. "More constraints."

"I'm just—" Z cut himself off, and we lapsed once more into uneasy silence.

My phone buzzed. My *actual* phone, not the decoy I'd carried ever since Richard took my phone, and that I'd been relieved of earlier.

It was a text, one word, from Derek. *Here.*

I paused, thinking, fingers hovering above the touch-screen. Then, using Z as cover, I composed a reply.

FOURTEEN

THERE WAS MUFFLED SHOUTING BEHIND THE DOOR to the warehouse antechamber.

The two guards covering said door gave it concerned glances, then, nodding at each other, turned around and raised their weapons.

The shouting stopped, replaced by grim silence.

Then the door *exploded* outward with a thunderous crash.

"Down! Down on the ground!"

"Drop your weapon or we shoot!"

Luckily, the warehouse guards had a pragmatic streak, and obeyed immediately.

Through the shattered door walked two men and

a woman, moving in professional formation past the shelving into the main area. Their eyes swept and analyzed the room—two guards (down), a crowd of civilians (panicking), and a team of doctors (unfazed and still working).

I recognized them at once.

Derek didn't acknowledge me at all—but it was better that way. Why give people a reason to connect me with the intruders? It might encourage them to come after me later, and I *really* didn't want that.

Instead, he addressed the room in a voice that carried effortlessly to the warehouse's four corners, despite sounding like pleasant conversation.

"Good evening," he said. "I and my comrades mean you no ill will, and will happily depart once I have what we came for. I'd advise against resistance— In the interest of preventing it, I'll happily disclose that members of your security are loyal to me, and will make those loyalties immediately apparent in the event of a firefight."

The two guards on the ground exchanged suspicious looks.

"Furthermore, provoking a firefight will draw law enforcement to this area. I think they'll be interested by the discrepancy between this warehouse's purported use, and the use to which it's currently being put. This must be why your security staff is forbidden from ever actually discharging their weapons."

That was a guess, but a safe one—and if correct, it reinforced Derek's earlier (false) claim of having friends among their ranks. I'd deemed it an acceptable risk in the hasty plan we'd concocted.

Derek sighed theatrically. "Such is the cost of business in such a robust neighborhood. And again, I apologize, but there's really no way around this. A young woman was injured in a fight here approximately twenty minutes ago. That woman is of my organization, and participated in that fight without my approval. She's mine to deal with, and I'll be taking her with me."

No fewer than three of the doctors attending

Kira stood up in protest, but the woman—Hanna, if I remembered right—gestured with her gun, and their protests died silent deaths. Personal danger outweighed the Hippocratic Oath, it seems.

"Her decision to participate was her own, and for that, I do not blame you," said Derek, his voice now slightly edged. "But the match was an unfair one, devised to be fatal. In it, she incurred injuries, which will keep her off active duty for the foreseeable future. Her replacement will not come cheap. I trust you'll agree that it would be *perfectly reasonable* for your organization to pay."

He nodded at the man to his right—Josh, Jeff, J-*something*—and he started toward the betting counter. Nobody tried to stop him.

"In the interest of fairness, I'll take only as much money as is owed the crowd as a result of Anna's victory . . . the victory you claim as invalid." We'd decided fake names for everyone involved was the way to go—for all their current handicaps, this was a powerful, organized force, and it'd both want vengeance for our actions, and be significantly more capable of harm in a different venue. "Anyone who comes forward with a winning stub will receive ten percent of their winnings—more than you'll get from *them.*"

That was my signal to approach and hand over my stub. A few others did too, but most stayed put, probably not willing to risk any potential backlash for a mere ten percent of their original bet. I wasn't too pleased with that risk myself. But caught between these guys and the Mafia, I really only had one choice.

Derek and J-something loaded the money into large black duffels while Hanna pointed her gun and glared at anyone who looked like they might try and interfere. When they'd finished, Derek spread his arms magnanimously.

"Thank you for your cooperation."

They walked back over to Kira's body and shooed away the doctors. J-something lifted her tenderly.

"Of course, we'll be taking hostages to ensure we aren't followed." Derek made a show of looking around the room before pointing at myself and Z. "You and you. Come on, then."

It was a transparent ploy made even worse by nobody in the warehouse having any reason to care what happened to us. But it might fool *somebody*.

We played our parts through for that chance's sake, protesting, blustering, bargaining, even some sobbing. But Derek, ever the hardhearted professional, brushed our pleas aside.

"Well, if I've gotta, could I at least have my phone back? That guy took it." I gestured at the supine culprit. Beside me, Z made affirmative noises.

Derek nodded slowly. "You heard the guy. Give me their phones. No sudden movements, now."

The bouncer complied, sliding Z's phone and then mine across the floor to Derek's feet. Derek scooped them up and motioned us toward the blasted door.

The team's fourth member was covering T-shirt lady and a couple others I didn't recognize. Upon seeing Derek, he snapped a crisp salute and fell into place within the formation.

Once we were far enough away to talk freely, Derek let out a loud whistle. "Damn. That was far above my pay grade. We're bodyguards, not SEAL Team Six."

"You're mercenaries," I said patiently. "Take the hazard pay from whatever we have over six million. And thank you."

"Hey, no prob. Just don't make a habit of it."

"Yeah, about that . . . " I hedged. "I might need something similar pretty soon."

Derek pursed his lips thoughtfully. "Christ. Fine. At least we have a little warning this time. What do you need?"

"I'll let you know when I've finalized the details . . . but I have a feeling it'll be a large-scale operation."

Derek looked the opposite of reassured.

They gave us a lift to Kira's car in their van. We still didn't have the key, but I'd (reluctantly) called Addie away from her job with a text explaining the situation. She wasn't happy about abandoning her position—I wasn't either—but this was an emergency of the highest priority. She was en route to Kira's in an Uber to grab the Applewoods' spare key. While we waited, we could decompress inside thanks to Hanna, who'd easily cracked the locks.

We split the duffels of money—big bricks of hundreds—and there it was, the payout Kira'd almost died for. Despite everything that'd gone wrong, *this* part of the Op was at least intact. Then we said our goodbyes to Derek and his squad—they'd been offsite long enough.

Now it was just us three—me in the driver's seat, Z in the passenger's, and Kira stretched out in the back. Z broke the silence first. "That's my cousin's job you just busted up."

The hostility was back in his voice. He stared out the window at the mostly-deserted parking garage.

I sighed. "Yeah, sorry about that. It's the only way I could think of to get Kira and the money."

"Nah, it's my fault. I knew something like this'd happen the moment you got involved."

Enough was enough.

"Wanna explain again how this is *my* fault?" I scoffed. "Obviously, I should've realized Little Miss Anger Problems'd arranged an impossible match behind my back. Ignore my *golden* plan that easily would've worked and blame me for everything. Again."

My voice was rising slowly. "And let's not forget why we were there at all. Because you didn't scrap your shitty plan like *I* advised. I was just dealing with *your* fuckup!"

"You didn't see a problem with—"

"Honestly, dude? I didn't fucking look that hard. Oh! Before I forget, we only took money your cousin's job should've paid out anyway, if they weren't such asshole cheapskates. And we only busted it to save Kira from the murderer they sent in to kill her. That's on them, not me. All I did was *save* us. Like I always do!"

"Yeah, save me, Jason Jorgensen!" spat Z. "Save me from the shitbox my life's been since you entered it!"

"Sure, blame me for that too! Keep pretending *I* sent—" . . . *Your dad upstairs*, I finished in my head.

179

But I didn't say it. I wasn't *that* injudicious, even as mad as I was.

The air sizzled between us, raw and dangerous. But abruptly, while we glared, the tension drained away as we remembered our current situation. Arguing was a luxury we couldn't afford, however badly we wanted to lay into each other. We were just two scared teenagers in a parking garage with a critically injured friend, and we needed each other, because that was all we had.

"I'll call an ambulance," said Z, sounding just as embarrassed as I felt.

"N'ambulance," came a croaky voice from the backseat.

I jumped, I'll admit—but you should've heard Z's little screech. Even when I processed what was going on, I *still* didn't believe it. But sure enough, when I looked into the backseat, Kira's eyes were open, despite all common sense saying otherwise.

"You're probably dying," said Z. "Even if you ain't, you've been hurt bad."

Kira shook her head weakly. "I'm fine."

It was so obviously untrue, I would've laughed if the situation weren't so serious.

"No, you're not," said Z. "You look like shit."

"I'm *fine*," Kira insisted, putting some edge into it.

"If you're fine, sit up."

Kira glared at Z. "Don' feel like it."

Z pulled out his phone.

"*Wait,*" said Kira. "Can' go. Cops."

"You remember what happened, then?" I asked, and Kira smiled weakly. "Yeah."

She was right. I gave it ninety percent odds that Peter Storm's thugs were actively looking for Kira right now. Checking the hospitals was the obvious move. If they found her . . . well, the nicest thing we could hope they'd do was turn her in for manslaughter.

"Hospital's out," I said.

"Are you *crazy?*" exploded Z. The anger from before was back, but I refused to get drawn in again. It'd been a mistake last time too.

"Think, dude. You run illegal fights. Everything's great until someone dies. Now you've gotta explain the death, because people're gonna miss him, and you can't just say, "Oh, he died in this illegal ring I run." You need a story. And if you set up the actual killer to take the fall, it dissuades people from making lethal accidents in the future. And where'll they look for her? The hospital." It felt weird talking so casually about the event in front of Kira, but I doubted she cared.

"Then what's your suggestion, O wise one? Her house? Looking like *this?*"

Kira shook her head urgently and then winced. "Ow."

"No, not home either." I pondered our options. "Z, you know any doctors? One who'd work secretly and privately—retired, maybe. We could drop her there, tell her parents we decided to go on a spontaneous road trip or something stupid like that."

"That . . . just might work," said Z slowly. "Yeah, there's a few people I could ask."

"No," came Kira's voice from the backseat again. "Can't. You need me. You know, for the . . ."

"That's true," I said.

Z looked like he wanted to rip the car into baseball-sized chunks and throw every last piece at my head. "The hell? No way she's doing that. Weren't you watching? She's—"

"He was watching, yeah. Watching me *kick ass*," said Kira. She sounded better than she had even seconds ago. "I could still kick yours too. Come at me."

Z ignored her. "Just change the plan."

"We'll see what your friend says," I said firmly. "If it's bad, I'll figure something out. But it's life and death. We're dealing with the mob here."

Z didn't look convinced.

"I'll give her as much time to heal as possible," I said, and Z just shook his head. Something was twitching in his jaw.

"You don't even care."

He opened the passenger door and got out, slamming it behind him.

"He couldn't stop me if he wanted to," said Kira with a weak laugh. "Glad you got my back, Jace."

"Uhhh . . . " There was so much I wanted to say—mostly variations on "you shouldn't be talking right now, let alone conscious." But she'd probably take that as a challenge, and everything else could wait until she wasn't half-dead. So for now . . .

"Go to sleep, Kira."

"Sure thing, boss," she said, and closed her eyes.

I hesitated only briefly before opening my own door and walking around the hood to find Z sitting against the front wheel. He glanced up as I approached, then looked down again without reacting. Taking this to be a good sign, I sat.

"Holy shit," he said at last.

"Holy shit," I agreed. "Holy fucking shit."

"She's crazy. She was smiling about all the ass she'd kicked, and she'd almost died, and she *killed someone*, dude. How could she . . . ?"

"Maybe she doesn't remember that part," I said, but we both knew I didn't believe that. Z was probably wondering now how dumb I thought he was. "She needs help," he said at last. "A doctor."

"No shit."

"You know what I meant."

"I do. Again, no shit."

I leaned back against the hood, stared at the green-tiled garage wall, and wondered if everyone else's life was as surreal as mine. "We'll get her help," I promised. "We'll wrap up this thing with the mob, then we can focus on our own lives a bit. I'll shoot her with a tranq-dart and drag her to a psychiatrist myself if I have to."

But Z didn't seem interested in talking anymore, so I let the conversation drop and busied myself with getting updates from Addie.

"Addie's on her way," I said some time later. "You find someone?"

"I did. He ain't happy I won't answer his questions.

Figured we could explain in person. But he'll do it. He's expecting us at his place."

"Great," I said with a genuine smile. "Really great. Hey Z, you, ah—" The words caught in my throat. "You like her, right?"

Z froze. Then he smiled too, but it was a melancholy, sardonic sort of smile. "I dunno," he said, voice heavy with tiredness. "I just don't anymore."

"I'm sorr—"

"Whatever."

I kinda wanted to hug him. But I'm not generally a very huggy person, and he wouldn't appreciate it, probably. So instead, I walked around behind the car, and threw open the trunk.

The trunk-light gleamed off of four black duffels, stuffed full with more money than the average person saw in a lifetime.

I opened my phone's camera settings.

"We got the cash," I said. "Let's show the mob we mean business."

FIFTEEN

ACCORDING TO DR. BERGMAN (OR, AS HE INSISTED we call him, Isaac), Kira's survival was the result of divine intervention. His documentation of her bodily injuries was thirteen pages even in his small, cramped shorthand, and his frequent updates on her status contained scary-sounding phrases like *severe abdominal contusions* and *costochondral separation* and *ISS Score of forty-one*. Once he was convinced his patient wouldn't die if he turned his attention elsewhere, he made it very clear she'd been exceptionally lucky, and that she'd need at least six months of intensive care and physical therapy before she was fit for release—preferably in an actual hospital, not the makeshift operating room he'd thrown together in his garage.

Lorenzo Michaelis'd insisted the handoff take place in three days.

I didn't feel comfortable going without Kira.

Kira'd stated she was coming, and the resulting argument between herself and Dr. Bergman'd almost got him shouting at his own patient.

When she'd finally convinced him she'd be leaving in three days regardless of his approval, he'd given in. He made some calls and soon, two *more* doctors'd arrived on his doorstep—one to switch off with Dr. Bergman in eight-hour shifts while the other sorted through a list of Kira's injuries, found treatments, and sorted them by priority based on time, short-term effectiveness, and necessity. They were made aware of the importance of secrecy, and I hoped they'd take it to heart. Given what I was paying them, they'd *better*.

If Dr. Bergman hadn't been single and childless, the situation would've been untenable.

As far as the Applewoods—Kira's parents and her

two younger sisters Anays and Emma—knew, Kira was touring the Great Lakes with us. They weren't happy she'd taken off without telling them, but imagine their reaction if we'd been truthful. *Hello, your daughter got into street fighting and almost died in the ring against a guy three times her size . . .*

They'd never let her so much as leave the house again.

Three days later, Kira'd stood shakily on her own two feet and given the trio of doctors a thumbs-up.

"I'm good," she'd said, which was so patently false that all three were struck speechless by her sheer audacity.

But there was no arguing with her, Hippocratic Oath be damned, and after she'd threatened to, "Put you in your own fucking hospital"—and demonstrated a certain amount of mobility, mobility all three experts agreed was "impossible"—they'd agreed to let her visit her parents, provided she returned within the day and promised to call if *anything* started feeling worse.

She'd promised, no doubt crossing her fingers behind her back.

And then we'd bundled into the car and most definitely *not* driven to Kira's house. We had a meeting in the Catskill Mountains, which was intensely odd, but the location hadn't been negotiable. We'd had the date since the mob wrote it in blood on Z's wall, but not the meeting place or time until the day of. We didn't get a *specific* area until five-thirty, a half-hour before the scheduled meet—Lorenzo didn't want us scouting the area beforehand.

Lorenzo Michaelis. *Il Diavoletto.*

I'd hoped to never have business with him again. Not that I'd ever *seen* him. My first, last, and only negotiation with the Bonannos'd been through the *valchiria*—Lorenzo's cadre of elite bodyguards, all women. According to Addie's intel, his enemies' tendency to underestimate them was a significant tactical advantage. In his correspondence with me, he'd indicated he'd be bringing two of them, and that I could bring two people of my own, but no more.

What few firsthand accounts we could gather painted him as a patient, intellectual, capable man with a famously cheerful disposition . . . which vanished immediately if he perceived an insult or a threat. Then his face would freeze over, and his ruthless streak would rise to the surface.

He possessed a sense of honor that seemed consistent (albeit unorthodox in its application), a sense of humor with similar qualifications, and a sense of vengeance a mile deep.

He was also healthy amounts of paranoid, so I heard, trusting only a few capos with sensitive matters. The only people he seemed to trust implicitly were his *valchiria*, who were tasked with his protection—and even then, he preferred to use them as emissaries. It was by only revealing himself when he deemed it safe that he'd stayed at the top as long as he had.

This was the man I was meeting. To turn over the seven million dollars we owed, shake hands, and walk away.

Of course, if that's all he wanted, I could've

dropped the money somewhere in the city and told him the location. There was no reason for a face-to-face meeting in the mountains . . . unless Lorenzo was planning something else.

I strongly suspected this *something else* involved dead teenagers, and had planned accordingly.

Kira's eyes—less swollen now, but certainly not fully healed—were fixed on the road, which twisted its way up the tree-covered mountainside. Z had shotgun. He kept glancing at her furtively. I don't think she noticed.

I was in the backseat. As usual.

Addie was again elsewhere, this time making sure my plan to deal with the Mafia went smoothly. Her absence felt *weird*, even though she'd only recently joined the team. It was like phantom limb syndrome, except instead of a limb, it was *Addie*—I can't explain it any better. And it didn't help my anxiety that she had the most dangerous job. Kira, though, didn't seem bothered at all.

"Just like old times," she'd said, seeing the three-person team. "The original gangsters. The OGs."

I'd debated with myself for several nights about whether I should cut or minimize Kira's role. It was clear to everyone—well, everyone but *her*—she wasn't fit for anything but extended hospital care. But then, even as battered as she was, there's nobody I'd rather have at my back.

In the end, the decision'd been simple, because Kira'd made it for me. Whatever bout of self-control she'd wrestled with in Vegas lay subdued at her feet, and seemed unlikely to return.

Whatever she'd experienced in that arena, she wanted more.

For most people, suffering injuries that serious would've woken them to their own mortality. Judging from Kira's driving, she wasn't most people. In fact, she might've concluded she was invincible and no longer had to worry about petty things like car crashes . . . much to the discomfort of the mere mortals riding with her.

"Shouldn't we take these turns a little slower?" I asked.

Kira shrugged. Our speed remained unchanged.

"It's just, I dunno if I can see the turn at this speed."

"Look faster."

"That doesn't even make sense."

Kira chuckled. "Arguing with cripples isn't cool."

"You're not—"

"Sounds like you were gonna argue."

Z sighed, exasperated.

"There," I said a bit later. "I think that's the rock."

Kira hit the brakes. The car skidded to a halt. "Where?"

"Behind us a bit. If we'd been going slower—"

We reversed slowly until the rock I'd seen reentered my vision. "That one."

Z squinted. "There's moss on it, but is it really *mossy*? Maybe there's an even mossier one later."

"Right turn at the mossy rock," I muttered. "Great

directions, Lorenzo. Well, let's try it. We've got some moss on a rock—how about a right turn?"

Kira pointed, and I followed her finger to the edge of the road. Now that she'd shown me where to look, I could see the beginnings of a dirt road that seemed to vanish as it curved steeply down the mountain-slope.

"Great," said Z. "Of all the things I wanted to do today, driving off a cliff was definitely near the top."

"Well, we'll be near the *bottom* soon enough," joked Kira, to loud groans. "Tough crowd, huh? Fine."

She changed into first gear. "Strap in tight. This could get bumpy."

With that, she twisted the wheel and inched the car forward onto the little strip of dirt. Slowly, painstakingly, we began down the steep, meandering (and incredibly scenic) side road. Not that we could appreciate it in our current frame of mind.

"I didn't know cars could *do* this," I said, clutching the driver's seat like it'd protect me if the wheels gave way and sent us spinning down to crash at the bottom of the valley.

"You just gotta treat them right," said Kira, who was suddenly driving very responsibly. "Getting out fast'll be a bitch, though. If they close the road, impossible."

"They won't."

Slowly, the road leveled off and started winding through the valley. "We've gotta be close," I commented, fighting back the doubt suddenly wrapping around my chest. This could go wrong so many ways. We were separated from our allies, in the middle of nowhere with a ruthless crime syndicate carrying a grudge against us. And the one of us tough enough to fight if necessary was sidelined until further notice—

"One sec," said Kira, pulling over. "Gotta take my pills."

—Not to mention currently high on painkillers.

There were better places to be, is what I'm getting at.

"Remind me why we're letting her drive again?"

said Z as Kira stuck a tablet in her mouth and followed it up with a big gulp of water.

I sighed. "Because she—"

"I'm a better driver smashed than you are sober," said Kira. "Better than both of you. Like, if you both were in the driver's seat and each holding the wheel . . ."

"We'd crash," I said. "Two people steering doesn't let you steer twice as well. It's like two people playing Mario Kart while each holding half the controller. There's no coordination."

"Exactly," said Kira. "You admit I'm better than both of you put together."

She pulled back onto the dirt road. "I know my limits, 'kay? I know what I can handle."

Her sudden vehemence caught me off guard and I let the matter drop before an argument could flare up. Kira's volatility was one variable I didn't wanna throw into this messy-ass plan. At this point, letting her drive was probably *safer* than arguing.

Besides, I couldn't quite get Troglodyte's bleeding neck out of my mind's eye.

The trees opened up into a large dirt parking lot. It looked ill-maintained—weeds were starting to reclaim it for the forest, and I got the distinct impression it only occasionally saw humans.

Now was one of those occasions. A not-immediately-countable number of cars were parked around the lot, and clustered around them stood an array of black-suited men. I counted sixteen.

"Private meeting," spat Kira. "Personal bodyguard only."

"Relax," I said. "We knew this already."

Heads were lifting, looking toward us. Guns followed suit, tracked the car as Kira backed into a parking spot, keeping the car's nose pointed at the exit.

I put my phone and wallet in the glove box, then stepped out, palms up and open. Unthreatening. Kira and Z were quick to follow.

"Hey," I said, nodding at the suits. "I'm here to see Mr. Michaelis."

They stared back at us, lingering over Kira's bruised face. At a nod from one—a big bulldog of a man with slicked-back hair—six men detached from the group and started patting us down for weapons.

"I didn't expect this big a party," I said. "I was told to bring two bodyguards. I was under the impression that Mr. Michaelis'd do the same."

Nobody deigned to answer, too focused on the pat-down. Finally, satisfied, they nodded to Bulldog, the apparent leader.

"Car," he said, and one did a quick look through the windows, then popped the trunk.

All as I'd expected. But I couldn't let them know that—because then they might start asking themselves what else I knew. And how.

"Which one of you's Mr. Michaelis?" I asked. "We've got business."

Bulldog raised his phone. "They're clear, boss," he said. He listened for a second, then looked at me directly for the first time. "*Il Diavoletto* will arrive shortly. You remember yourself when talking, *capiche?*"

"I capiche," I said, beckoning Kira and Z beside me. Bulldog motioned his men back several steps, but they didn't lower their guns.

"I had lots to do today," I said to Kira. "Still haven't stocked up on cleaning supplies or spices, and I wanted to go birthday shopping for Jeeves. But I decided to come here instead. Starting to regret that choice."

"Why, does our company suck that much?" said Kira with a grin. Always up for some good banter, that was Kira.

"It's more the semi-automatic weapons being leveled at us by enough gangsters to stage a musical."

"Yeah, I see that."

" . . . Though you could *also* be better company."

I squinted around the valley, at the trees, the vines, the mountain-slopes. I couldn't see any snipers, but I knew where they'd be placed, from a tactical perspective. One team on that outcropping, one with a clear path between the trees . . .

The sky really *was* exceptionally blue today. It was an aesthetic observation, but also a tactical one. The sun had a few hours of light left before dusk.

Lorenzo wouldn't wait until dusk. He had the advantage in light. We'd entered his trap, and he wouldn't let us slip away under any circumstances. But he also couldn't resist a face-to-face meeting with the teenagers who'd become such a thorn in his side . . . and sure enough, an engine's familiar growl slowly rose in volume until a bright yellow Lamborghini emerged from the trees, coasted into the lot, and came to a graceful halt right in the entrance.

Because given the option, why *not* deny other cars passage? We weren't waiting on anyone else, after all.

I looked at the semicircle of men with guns and tried to remember the situation was under control.

The passenger door opened, and out stepped a very small man.

He couldn't have been more than five feet tall.

Slim too, so slim he could blow away in a strong wind. He carried a diamond-topped cane, sized to his height, and wore an Armani suit that must've been custom-fitted. The combined effect should've been comical, but there was something in the man's face that arrested judgment.

It was confidence born of utter control. *I can order you shot if I decide I don't like your tie*, said his eyes, and the curve of his lips, and the weight of his stance.

Nobody I'd talked to'd mentioned his size, and now I understood why. I could already tell that when I reflected on this meeting, I'd remember this man as at least five-foot-ten.

His gaze met mine and his smile widened. With small, fast strides, he closed the distance between us and extended an inviting hand.

"Hello, Mr. Jorgensen," said Lorenzo Michaelis, street boss of the Bonanno family. "I'm so happy to finally meet you in person."

SIXTEEN

GRASPED LORENZO'S HAND AND HIS FINGERS CLOSED around mine like five tiny vices. We shook twice, briskly.

"This is more than two bodyguards, Mr. Michaelis," I said. "I hope you aren't planning a double-cross."

Lorenzo smiled genially. "Not so, my friend. I am an honorable man. I said I would bring only two bodyguards . . . and I have."

He motioned to his car, from which two women were exiting—his *valchiria*. One was tall and well-built, with a hard expression and a tightly-wound brown bun. The other . . .

Addie Bristol stared at me sternly, without a flicker of recognition. I fought the urge to wink.

Lorenzo waved a ring-weighted hand. "These others here, I was not expecting them. They are friends of mine, but they are free to go where they please. I hope you do not mind?"

His smile'd become rather fixed, and as he awaited my answer, I noticed the tall woman's hand resting casually on her Beretta.

"Not at all," I said, swallowing. "You're a lucky man to have so many friends."

Lorenzo laughed at that. His eyes moved over Z and Kira. "These are the friends you brought?"

I nodded.

His eyes stopped on Kira and bored a hole in her bruise-mottled face. "You are called Queen Bitch, yes? Rumor was you'd died." He flicked some imaginary dirt from under his nail. "And many want it actualized. I've heard much about you, and if one-tenth is true, your skills are far beyond what Mr. Jorgensen deserves. Why not work for me? I can always use more *valchiria*."

Kira spat. Lorenzo sighed theatrically.

"Just as charming as I'd heard. *You* must be the late Mr. Davis's son." He inclined his head toward Z, whose fists were clenched so hard his knuckles'd bleached white. "Your first name is apparently widely debated. You were behind the latest Crip attempt on my life, yes? Don't bother answering—I'm correct."

He looked past Z to the car. "There is a fourth who keeps company among you."

"Not here," I said quickly. "I was told to bring two. I chose who I thought'd be most useful."

"I checked the car, boss," said Bulldog. "They came alone."

"Check again," said Lorenzo. "The fourth of their group is adept at going unseen. I want men covering the perimeter just in case. I will tolerate no slip-ups."

It was so, *so* hard to not look at Addie right then, but I somehow succeeded.

Bulldog returned to the car, opened the doors, windows, and trunk. Searched it clean through. Presumably finding nothing, he nodded at Lorenzo, who gave a satisfied smirk.

"Do you know why we are meeting here, beneath the trees?" he asked.

I had a decent guess, but I didn't wanna spoil his fun.

"Because your recent antics have clarified that you have no qualms about getting the police involved. You are not content to play the game honorably. I see the advantage—a rat being drowned will bite at its captor's hands—but have never understood such behavior myself. Nonetheless, you are dangerous . . . and require gloves. Now you see the need for isolation."

I did. What's more, I'd expected it—Addie'd slipped me this meeting-place two days ago, along with the number of deployed Mafiosos, the number and location of Lorenzo's snipers, and his plan of action.

It ended in our deaths, naturally. It always had. But Lorenzo Michaelis hadn't attained his current position by wasting potential resources. And we owed him seven million dollars . . .

"I am thoroughly up-to-date on the current state

of law enforcement in the area," said Lorenzo calmly. "Levels are normal—which is to say, minimal. The closest station is eighteen miles away. And I have posted watchers along the major roads to tell me if there is a sudden surge of activity. The emergency call is your greatest and only real weapon, and as you see, I have neutered it like a defiant bull." He snapped his fingers. "So there will be no tricks today. I would not be here were I concerned for my own safety, and I am not alive because I am under-cautious. Now, to the matter of payment for your treachery. Seven million dollars or your lives. And as you are not hiding, I conclude you have the money."

It *was* a decent plan, considering Lorenzo's knowledge of our current capabilities. Unfortunately for him, that left two major holes—holes that thanks to Addie's report, I'd been prepared to exploit.

First, nothing kept us from changing the rules, developing new tactics. Lorenzo's plan wasn't built around failsafes, unexpected occurrences, worst-case scenarios, but around stopping the strategy he thought we'd try. The easiest way around plans like that? Try something else.

Second, his sentries'd been ordered to report increased police activity. But they'd received no orders to report if activity *stayed constant*. Easily missable—why would Lorenzo care if nothing changed? But that lack of caring left a security flaw wide enough to fly a jet through.

For if Lorenzo didn't hear from his sentries, he assumed everything was still going as planned.

Things hadn't been going as planned for approximately two hours. He just didn't know it yet.

"All correct, Mr. Michaelis," I said. "On behalf of my subordinate, who wronged you and your organization, I'll pay what's owed. And erase our debts to the Bonanno family."

It was a question, and Lorenzo took it as one. "Correct."

That rotten little liar.

"Forgive me," I said. "I didn't realize the Mafia'd be so . . . understanding. I was gonna use the money as a bargaining chip for our lives if I had to. So it's kinda not with me."

Lorenzo nodded, like he'd expected that. "Where is it?"

"I dunno."

He raised an eyebrow.

"It was entrusted to my third colleague," I lied, "so I wouldn't reveal her location, or the money's, under duress. We have a code phrase . . . if I tell her everything's alright, she'll bring the money here."

It was actually safely hidden a few towns over—if something went wrong and Addie was discovered, I didn't wanna be down a bargaining chip. It probably wouldn't help much, but the chance was at least there.

Lorenzo smiled. "Make the call, then."

I patted my pockets. "I left my phone in the car."

"*Valchiria*, accompany Mr. Jorgensen to his car. If he attempts to do anything but retrieve his phone, stop him. Lethally."

Addie and the brown-bunned girl nodded simultaneously. It was incredibly creepy.

"I . . . " Hesitation. This was the hard sell. "I'm aware of your bodyguards' abilities, and won't accompany them without a guard of my own . . . for my safety."

Lorenzo sucked in a cheek. It'd be easy enough to refuse, given his superior position. And yet . . . if he did, would his *valchiria* appear weak if he didn't trust them to subdue some kids in a fight?

So fast I almost missed it, he looked at Kira. And then past her and up, to the snipers positioned in the bluffs. Why not humor me—what did he care? No matter what, we'd still be within the snipers' sights.

Or so he thought.

"You may keep your escort alongside mine. But raise a finger to one and your lives are forfeit."

"Understood," I gulped. I tried to make it big, like just considering the consequences unnerved me.

Four shadows followed me to the car. Kira stepped ahead and opened the driver's door. I climbed in and crawled over to the passenger side, then looked back.

The brown-bunned *valchiria* was watching me and frowning, like she expected me to produce a gun, or a bomb, or a jetpack. Kira and Z stood behind her. The keys still dangled from Kira's right hand. Behind them stood Addie, covering them with her Beretta.

I met her eyes. Three silent steps brought her directly behind the other woman.

"Don't move," she said calmly, shoving the gun into her lower back. Her voice was even, betraying no hint that she'd never taken a life and probably couldn't bring herself to. "Don't cry for help either, or I'll blow a bullet through your fucking guts."

The maneuver was invisible from Lorenzo's perspective . . . and those of his other men.

The *valchiria* froze, and didn't resist when Z removed the pistol and taser from her belt, using her body as cover from Lorenzo's view. She muttered a long string of Italian, and Addie responded in kind, too fast to follow.

I reached into the glove compartment and hefted my phone. The clock was ticking—if I stayed in the car too long, Lorenzo'd surely get suspicious. But I couldn't bring myself to continue. If something went wrong—

But that *possibility* was nothing to the certainty if I *didn't* act.

So I smashed my misgivings into a ball and swallowed them. And then I sent a quick text.

I wondered which of the five sniper nests contained the man I'd sent it to.

Each nest, Addie'd reported, contained three men—spotter, shooter, and someone watching another nest in case of attack. One would need all five locations, the ability to attack them simultaneously, and the skill to execute each attack with near-perfect timing to take them out.

Addie'd supplied the locations. I'd supplied the ability.

And Derek's mercenaries'd supplied the skill.

The message I sent him was one word long. *Showtime.*

A single shot split the air.

Lorenzo's men gasped, cried out, shouted orders—a mess of noise competing to be heard. Z fired his newly-acquired taser into its previous owner's front and she collapsed, twitching. Kira threw herself into the driver's seat, and Z and Addie climbed frantically into the back, but nobody was paying us any notice—they were under attack. And besides, they had a car blocking the driveway and five teams of snipers to shoot us down . . .

One of those was gone, and the others didn't matter. Kira let out a series of strained war-whoops as she floored the pedal, flattening the low wooden fence that separated the lot from the forest. We bounced a little going over the grass—Civics weren't built for off-road travel—but we cleared the parked Lamborghini.

Behind us, Lorenzo'd realized his snipers weren't shooting at us, and shouted orders. His men sprayed gunfire in our direction, but it was too late—bullets made *spanging* sounds against the Civic's metal, but lacked penetrating force at this distance.

The engine roared, and we left that deathtrap behind, traveling far too fast for the unkept mountain path. Any other time, I would've ordered Kira to ease up. Not now. Now, we needed speed. Because I'd ordered Derek not to kill anyone, and once Lorenzo's men realized they weren't being hit, they'd get in their cars and pursue.

Kira was laughing now, big, genuine laughter. Our speed slowed to a crawl as the road steepened, and she revved the engine louder to compensate.

There should've been guards on the road, making sure we couldn't come back up. But this too Addie'd warned us of, and another of Derek's teams'd struck at it preemptively. They hadn't even had time to close the gate. Kira passed through that particular checkpoint at thirty miles per hour.

Doesn't sound that fast, huh? Trust me—in the forest, it is.

Kira wrenched the wheel left as we crested the lip of the slope, narrowly saving us from becoming paste on the mossy boulder at the top.

We were probably being pursued. But that was no concern—Derek's crew'd taken out another critical part of Lorenzo's strategy en route to the nests.

The sentries.

As the familiar warble of police sirens grew in

volume, the car's stress level relaxed. Twenty seconds later, a line of twelve cop cars passed us going the other way.

And that, I hoped, was the end of our trouble with Lorenzo Michaelis.

"We fucking kicked their asses," said Kira, baring her teeth, once we were safely away.

"Showed them who's boss," grinned Z.

Even Addie allowed herself a smile.

But I couldn't quite share their joy. Because that's not a leader's job. Sure, they'll celebrate with the team, but being leader means constantly looking toward the future, only staying in the now long enough to secure it as a beachhead from which to launch other campaigns.

I was looking toward the future now, and I didn't like what I saw.

Addie noticed first, as always. She touched my shoulder gently from the backseat. "You alright?"

"We got Lorenzo. I assume we did, anyway. Probably a bunch of the Bonannos too. But the mob won't just ignore that. They'll take off the gloves and come after us in force."

It was the logical progression from where we'd escalated. But since the beginning, we'd never had a choice. It'd always been escalate or die . . . and now we'd escalated about as far as we could handle.

But the Mafia was capable of so much more. Lorenzo's presumed fall wouldn't even slow them down. It'd just invigorate them.

I'd known this, and I'd committed to the plan anyway. Because the alternative was dying without putting up a fight. And if you were still fighting, you could still win.

Perhaps I understood Kira a little better, thinking that. Perhaps we weren't so different. As long as we were alive, we'd keep fighting.

I took a deep breath, knowing nobody'd like this next part.

"We gotta skip town."